INDIAN FIGHTER

Center Point
Large Print

**This Large Print Book carries the
Seal of Approval of N.A.V.H.**

ॐ श्री गणेशाय नमः

E. E. HALLERAN

INDIAN FIGHTER

CENTER POINT PUBLISHING
THORNDIKE, MAINE

This Center Point Large Print edition
is published in the year 2002 by arrangement with
Golden West Literary Agency.

The text of this Large Print edition is unabridged.
In other aspects, this book may vary from the original
edition. Printed in Thailand. Set in 16-point
Times New Roman type by Bill Coskrey.

ISBN 1-58547-106-2

Cataloging-in-Publication Data is available from the Library of Congress.

CHAPTER 1

From the west the Laramie Mountains were not impressive. Viewers on the eastern prairie might see them as quite a range of hills but to the men of the eastbound mail escort they were just a minor barrier to be passed before hitting the long downgrade into the valley of the Platte. Once across the low divide which separated the Medicine Bow from the Laramie it would all be downhill. With luck the mail coach might get through before either Indians or snow could come along.

At the crossing of Foot Creek the wizened little driver pulled up, resting his horses for the haul over the second part of the divide. His lone passenger clambered out of the coach to give him a hand with watering the horses, both men willing enough to stretch cramped legs and restore circulation. The November wind had a nip in it and the dusty miles from crude little Fort Halleck had not been comfortable ones.

The coach was almost ready to roll again when a lean man in faded blue eased down the twisting slope that the mail coach was about to climb. He said nothing until he had swung from the saddle to drink thirstily at the tiny creek, the sweaty blue at the seat of his breeches standing out darkly against the dustiness of the rest of him as he bent over. While his equally dusty horse drank downstream a few feet the man untied the yellow bandana from his neck and used it to wash some of the alkali crust from the stubble of tawny beard. Then he rinsed the handkerchief and knotted it about his neck once more, trickles of water tracing dark furrows in the dust of his uniform blouse. He shivered a little at the chill of it and then he turned to aim a wry grimace at the stage driver.

"Seems like we got to make a choice, Hardhead," he said, his easy drawl carrying just a hint of the South in its breadth of vowel and slurring of the r's. "Been no rain worth talking about for a fortnight. Seems like the snow flurries last week didn't amount to much. Either trail ought to be all right."

The stage driver pulled off his flop-brim hat and wiped his forehead. "Hell, Sarge," he growled. "I ain't the one to decide. It's your dam' army that tells me what to do. When the orders said to stay away from the old Cherokee Trail I stopped figgerin'. It's up to you."

The soldier chuckled quietly, showing even white teeth behind the unshaven lips. He didn't mind hearing Hardhead Maginnis complain about army rules. Maginnis complained about everything. It was almost fun to hear him, and it was mildly entertaining to see him pull his hat off whenever he had half an excuse. Twice in the past three years the little driver had survived Indian attacks, each time suffering a minor head wound which left a bare patch on his round skull. Now he kept his gray hair close cropped so that the scars would show to advantage. He was proud of those bare spots, one from an arrow and one from a musket ball, just as he was proud of his new nickname. Hardhead was a better name than most of the ones he had been given during his long and unwashed career with horses.

The passenger broke in then, his manner as impatient as his words. "You'd better damned sight pick the right trail!" he snapped. "Sending this coach all the way up to Fort

Laramie is an outrage and using these unknown mountain trails is just as stupid. The least the army could have done was to send competent guides!"

Sergeant Barry eyed the man calmly. He took his time about it, rubbing comfortably at newly washed whiskers with a lean brown hand. It felt so good to be rid of the alkali dust that he couldn't even get sore at the stout man's tone. Finally he said casually, "Mister Rossiter, the army's always got a reason for what it does. Sometimes the reason don't make much sense—but there's still a reason." He let his drawl take on a little extra breadth as he spoke, partly because he had detected a similar drawl hidden behind the ill-humor in the other man's words.

Rossiter refused to be soothed. No taller than the stage driver he carried a hundred pounds more on his small frame and still managed not to seem particularly comic. Even the pointed brown beard which did not conceal the extra chins was not funny. Somehow, the man gave the impression that he could be pretty dangerous if he wanted to be. Certainly he was not backward about showing a pompous anger at people who didn't do things the way he wanted them done. "I took passage to Denver," he said in the same angry voice. "I'm far behind schedule already due to endless army delays and pettifogging. Now this change of trail! I consider it inexcusable stupidity on the part of your militia officers to send this coach so far from its established route."

"Don't blame the militia—or any other officers," Barry told him, still keeping his own voice easy. "Orders came from higher up. They decided to abandon the Mormon and Oregon Trails when the Sioux started raiding two years ago. Now the Cheyennes have been hitting the Overland and the South Platte. So we change trails again. Don't think we like it any better than you do." He was thinking to himself that Rossiter's impatience was no greater than his own.

"Still nonsense!" the fat man said, glowering. "You can't hide from an Indian by taking to the woods!"

"The army keeps trying," Barry replied. "Like I said, their reasons don't always make much sense. Let's go, Hardhead."

As he swung into the saddle he heard the driver explaining to his irate passenger that the commander at Fort Laramie had only ninety men to do the work of guarding a good five hundred miles of dangerous trails. Not to mention the telegraph lines.

"We'll head for the Sybille Creek Trail, Maginnis," Barry called back over his shoulder. "They say it's not so rocky as the one along the Laramie River."

Maginnis waved acknowledgment but Rossiter's voice snarled a reply to what the driver had been saying. "Ninety men! You mean ninety thugs. I've heard about the kind of men the government has left in the forts out this way. Turn-coat secessionists, draft dodgers and the real scum of the frontier! No wonder we keep running from the Indians!"

Sergeant Barry urged his horse to the climb from the creek bottom, his wave to Maginnis an order to get started. "Come on, Hardhead. The scum ought to have the pass scouted by this time."

He choked back his anger at Rossiter, putting his mind to the job ahead. At the top of the first rise he paused to glance in all directions, exchanging signals with men who had climbed the ridge on either side of the winding trail. Riding

8

guard over a stage coach was a trick which Tom Barry had learned the hard way. A mere escort of armed men offered no protection against the kind of raids the Sioux and Cheyennes had been staging. The target simply became larger and more tempting. Barry made every mail detail a sort of scouting expedition, his men moving as skirmishers in position to give warning of danger before an enemy could get to close quarters. Troopers under his orders grumbled at the hard riding but there was a ring of pride in their grumbles. In November of eighteen sixty-four there were not many mail details that had lost neither a man nor a coach. Barry's squad could claim that distinction.

The lean sergeant climbed again, satisfied that things were going according to custom. Marcel Ladou, the former Louisiana Tiger, was pushing his way through the scattered pines which sprinkled the ridge north of the trail. At about the same distance to the south Gerhardt Strauss, reputedly a deserter from the Austrian Imperial Guard, was executing the same kind of flanking movement. Back at the creek Ben Samuels would be watering his horse after having kept an eye on the crossing until the coach was safely on its way. Barry could only guess at the present position of his advance scout but he didn't worry on that score. A man who had served his apprenticeship with Jim Bridger didn't need a Tennessee sergeant to tell him his business.

It took a good half hour to climb into the pass and by that time the two out-riders had moved back to the trail, forced in by converging rock walls. Barry left them riding just ahead of the coach while he went forward at a faster pace, guessing that Sawdust would now have something to say about the next stage of the journey. While there had been no report of hostiles in the Laramie Mountains, conditions might change at any time. The tribes had been three years in discovering that the big war in the east had drawn most of their white soldier enemies from the forts and left only puny garrisons scarcely capable of defending the posts themselves and a bit of trail. Now they seemed to have gotten fully awake to the opportunity. The South Platte had been a bloody mess for almost four months. Denver was virtually cut off from the east. Mail service was being interrupted almost every week. No trail was safe from one day to the next.

As the trail flattened a little at the summit of the pass Barry began to look for signs of his advance man. Private Henry Featherstone—commonly known to his friends as Sawdust—would not have gone down into the valley of the Sybille without halting for some kind of report. He should be showing himself at any moment.

Instead there came a cautious hail. The scout's nasal voice called, "Dismount and git into the timber, Sarge. We got comp'ny ahead."

Barry swung away without hesitation, moving toward the sound of the voice as he led his horse into the timber. Featherstone was just beyond a thicket of pines, lounging comfortably against a tree with an enormous quid of tobacco distending one of the lean, leathery cheeks. He was tall, lanky, ungainly, and dirty, a streaked undershirt open down the front to show a thin but very hairy chest. The chest hair was black although the straggling fringe which showed beneath the broken blue forage cap was a sandy brown. One bony knee peeked through a huge rent in what had once been cavalry breeches. Private Featherstone was his usual meticulous self. By some quirk of wartime enlistment he was on the roster of the regular army, a fact which militia units accepted gratefully. They were often accused of not looking or acting like soldiers—but they didn't have anybody quite as disreputable as Sawdust Featherstone.

"Where?" Barry asked as he stopped beside the scarecrow.

"Down below." He gestured toward the Sybille valley.

"Indians?"

Sawdust displayed the remains of broken front teeth as he grinned amiably. "You was expectin' mebbe Quantrill's guerrillas?"

Barry matched the grin. In nearly three years of campaigning he and Featherstone had come to understand each other pretty well. "This fall it could be practically anybody. So tell it the way you saw it."

"Looks to me like a huntin' party blundered in here and happened to spot us," the lanky scout said slowly, the words half muffled behind the wad of tobacco. "I figger they was workin' the valley and one of 'em seen the coach comin' through the pass. Anyway, I was jest in time to see this polecat ridin' hell-bent down to where the others was a-loafin' around. I didn't git to see 'em fer long but I counted six. They ducked outa sight about that time so I ain't sure there wouldn't be more."

"They're laying an ambush?"

"Likely. Good spot fer it on them bluffs where the crick goes through the gorge."

"Sioux?"

Sawdust wagged his head slowly. "Funny thing about

that, Sarge. That fust one I seen was a Sioux sure as hell. He was closer'n any of them others. But later I got a look at the gang slippin' into the brush. I'd say there was Cheyennes among 'em."

"That sounds bad. So far they haven't been working together very much. This way they'll try to outdo each other in wiping us out."

"Come over this way a piece," Sawdust urged. "There's a rock where we kin see down into the valley."

Barry followed him to an outcrop which permitted him to stare down into the wooded valley of a winding creek. It was easy to spot the gorge Featherstone had mentioned but there was no sign of Indians.

"They're on top o' the cliffs," the scout asserted. "Waitin' fer us."

"You're sure?"

"I'd take odds if ye was givin' 'em. Or mebbe it's an even bet. I still figger they're a band that jest happened along but that don't keep 'em from gittin' ideas about skelps."

Barry studied the terrain carefully. That gorge would be the perfect ambush spot for the usual sort of guard detail. Coach and guards alike could be wiped out in no time. "Six of them, you said?"

"Six that I seen. They didn't act like they was meetin' any more."

Barry nodded. At times like this it was a good idea to take a Sawdust guess at its face value. The man might have a reputation as a trouble maker around a settlement or a fort but in the mountains he knew his business. "Maybe we can surprise them a mite."

Featherstone shifted his chew and grinned. "You thinkin'

12

what I'm thinkin'?"

"Likely. I learned this Indian fighting from you so I'll assume that you'd try to get them from the rear. And on both sides of the creek."

"That's the way I'd do it."

"Good. Which side do you want to take? You'll have to handle it alone. I've got to keep somebody with the coach."

"I'll git across the crick. I'll have more time than anybody else 'cause I kin start right now."

"Good. You've got a half hour to move into position above that far cliff. I'll bring Ladou with me and find a spot on the near side. All right with you?"

"Sure. But tell that damned Louisiana mush-rat where I'll be holed up. I don't want him shootin' at me by mistake. He's too damned good."

"Half hour," Barry repeated. "Get moving."

He hurried back to the trail in time to halt the coach before it could ease into the steep downgrade. Samuels was still out of sight in the rear but he explained the position quickly to the others. "Take it plenty slow going down. Give Marcel and me a chance to get set. Gerhardt rides out ahead so they'll see him and think he's the regular lead scout. If Samuels gets close enough to do any talking tell him to stick close. And don't get within rifle range of that gorge!"

He motioned for the swarthy Ladou to follow him and the pair plunged directly into the heavier stand of pines which flanked the trail on the north. There was no time to waste now. He had cut it fine with his guess of a half hour and he didn't want to risk a delay which might cause the savages to alter their plans. Better to hit them while their intentions were clear and their position known.

They dismounted before they reached the bottom of the slope, leading their horses until they found level ground. Then they tied the animals to pines and moved forward again, Barry trying to get his bearings. The gorge had been evident enough from up there on the mountain but now the cliff tops must appear as just part of the valley floor. Finally he worked it out just as a grunt from Ladou confirmed that they were heading in the right direction. Four Indian ponies were tethered in the trees a little distance to their left.

"Real easy now," he whispered to the Cajun. "We'll close in a mite but we don't make any real move until the coach shows on the lower trail. That's when I figure the Cheyennes and the Sioux might try to out-maneuver each other so as to get first crack at the victims. When they move for better positions we let 'em have it. Understand?"

"Bien," Ladou grinned, the expression almost hidden beneath the sweeping black mustache with its burden of alkali dust. "They weel be ver-ry surprise, no?"

"You better hope they will. We're outnumbered two to one. And don't try to depend too much on that rifle of yours. At close quarters you'd better rely on that Officers' Model Colt you stole at Fort Halleck."

The big fellow grinned sheepishly, this time seeming to roll back the mustache to let strong white teeth show. He pulled a Colt's revolver from inside his uniform blouse and became very intent on checking its loads and primers. Then he grinned at Barry again. "Ver-ry good guns in this army, no?"

"Very good guns yes. Make sure you use them good."

Two minutes later they saw the coach coming down into

the valley, a ramrod-stiff figure riding ten yards ahead of the team. Private Strauss was putting on his best Grenadier Guard performance but his carbine was held ready across the saddle in front of him. On the coach weapons also were in evidence. Rossiter had climbed to the seat beside Maginnis, a rifle across his knees while another weapon was wedged between the two men. They were ready but they showed no signs of nervousness.

"Now move in," Barry ordered. "Easy. They should be getting edgy any minute now."

They had crawled forward a dozen yards, studying the undergrowth which fringed the top of the cliff, when suddenly a carbine banged somewhere across the gorge. Sawdust had opened the fight.

CHAPTER 2

Instantly there was action on the near side of the gulch. Two brown forms came up out of hiding places to scream angry questions across the ravine. Barry lined his sights on the nearer savage, firing almost in the same instant that Ladou did. That brought real uproar. A rifle cracked sharply across the creek and somewhere the duller boom of a musket backed it up. Angry, startled yells mingled with the hoarse sound of somebody cursing in German. Private Strauss was driving in, firing and cursing as he came. Across the creek the carbine slapped again and nearer at hand a musket blasted.

By that time an Indian was breaking out of the thicket directly in front of Barry, running toward the spot where the Indian ponies had been left. Barry was just drawing his revolver and he was a little slow in getting it into use, his shot missing as the warrior disappeared into thicker timber. Then another Indian came in from an angle; Barry whirled just in time to duck the tomahawk that was aimed at his head. He fired point blank with the revolver, knowing that Ladou had fired at almost the same moment. The Indian fell in a sprawling heap almost at his feet, an unused musket plowing up the carpet of pine needles as it fell.

A sudden silence was broken only by the continuing volley of teutonic curses and the clatter of unshod hoofs in the lower valley. Barry guessed that one Indian had escaped on each side of the gulch. "Move up to the rim," he ordered, noting that the Cajun had reloaded his favorite rifle. "Take it easy. We're not sure Sawdust counted all of them."

He shouted a warning to the scout as they approached the cliff top. Replies came from both Sawdust and Strauss. The ambush had been completely smashed. Not a single shot had been fired at the mail coach which was now coming slowly into the ravine. There had been no casualties among the men of the mail guard. The amazing record of the detachment was still perfect.

"Keep moving," Barry yelled at Maginnis when the coach drew even with his position. "We'll make sure we didn't miss any. Samuels! Ride on ahead with Strauss. Keep your eyes open for two Indians who got away. We'll take care of the rear while we're getting caught up to you."

He went back to stare grimly at the two warriors that had fallen first. Both were Cheyennes and both were dead. There was nothing unusual about either so he went into the brush to look at the one who had thrown the hatchet at him.

16

This one he could not identify. The moccasins were different in pattern and style from any he had ever seen, the soles not having the nearly straight instep line which was so typical of both Sioux and Cheyenne footgear. Nor were they like anything he had noticed on Pawnees, Arapahos, or Kiowas.

Ladou stooped to pick up the dead Indian's musket. Now he handed it over. "We see these many time before, no?" he commented with a crooked smile. "What you theenk?"

The weapon was an Enfield musket of the type that had been issued to so many Confederate regiments in the early days of the war. Barry made no reply but rolled the dead Indian over to study the beadwork on the parfleche which had been partly concealed. The beadwork was also strange, but the cartridge box beside it was quite familiar. It was nearly new and bore the letters C.S.A.

A hail from Sawdust interrupted them. The lanky scout came up at one end of the bluff, a broad grin making the tobacco-packed cheek look more lopsided than ever. "Seems like I didn't do too damned good on my side, Sarge. Wasn't but two o' the bastards over there and I let one of 'em git away."

"We let one slip through," Barry told him quietly. "But take a look at this fellow. What do you make of him?"

The scout hunkered down to make a careful examination of the beadwork on belt and leggings. "It was a Sioux I kilt," he said casually as he worked. "Dunno about the one what got away. Never seen him real good."

"Cheyennes on this side," Barry replied. "Except for this one."

Sawdust studied the painted face of the dead warrior.

Then he poked gingerly at the medicine bag which was on a bit of rawhide around the twisted neck. "I make him a Delaware," he said finally. "Ain't many of 'em git out this way. Them as does generally gits theirselves skelpt by the Sioux. Damned funny, I'd call it."

Barry motioned toward the musket and the cartridge box. "Seems like somebody will be interested in this."

The scout looked up quickly, first at Barry and then at the silent Ladou. "Throw 'em away," he suggested. "You fellers are the only two Galvanized Yanks in the outfit. No point in stirrin' up any more talk against ye. Me, I won't say a damned word."

"Let's have a look at the ponies," Barry suggested without replying to the suggestion. "I don't think the fellow who got away had time to cut loose any of the other horses."

They found three ponies still tied in the thicket. Two of them were just Indian ponies with rawhide hackamores and frayed blankets on their backs in place of saddles. The third one was more gaudily decorated and had an army bedroll and slicker behind the riding blanket. Sawdust unfastened the roll and spread it, all three watchers noting the C.S.A. stamped on the gray blanket. Then the interest turned to a curiously notched stick about eighteen inches long. It had once been a simple piece of lodgepole pine, peeled but not otherwise shaped very much. Now it was covered with notches and cuts which turned two thirds of its length into strange scrollwork. At the smooth end another groove encircled the wood but this cut had an obvious purpose. It served as a place to tie a dirty bit of red silk ribbon which formed a handle loop. Barry wondered briefly what emigrant woman had lost her life when the Indians became the owners of that ribbon.

"What is it?" he asked as Sawdust hesitated.

"Ole Jim Bridger useta call 'em count-sticks. There's an Injun name but I don't know what it is. I ain't sure how to read these things but Bridger useta say that an Injun with a count stick was better'n a white man with a notebook. And more likely to be tellin' the truth."

"But what's the point of it?"

"Scouts used 'em. Bridger said a scout could ease through another tribe's huntin' ground and come back with real good figgers on what villages were in the country and how many fightin' men was in every one of 'em."

"Then somebody's been taking a sort of Indian census?"

"Looks that way. Some o' these marks mean tribes. That much I know. The rest of it's countin'. I'd figger this here Delaware was out tryin' to round up the tribes in this part o' the country. The stick is his report of how many warriors outa each batch he figgers will sign up."

Barry didn't need to ask questions about what it meant that such a tally should be in progress. Since the very beginning of the war there had been wild rumors about the Confederate government trying to raise the Indians against the frontier posts. Lately these rumors had been getting wilder, partly because of the rash of Cheyenne raids along the Platte but also because there was evidence that a Confederate agent had actually been working among the Kiowas and Comanches. People in fear of their lives didn't need much of a hint to let their fears increase.

"Sounds bad," he said grimly. "I suppose he was on his way back to wherever he came from, escorted by a sort of honor guard of both Sioux and Cheyennes. They couldn't stand the temptation to pick up what looked like easy scalps."

"That's the way I figger it," Sawdust agreed. "Now what about this here count-stick? If we take it in to the fort it's goin' to stir up some mighty rough talk. You Rebs have been gittin' plenty o' dirty talk without givin' folks a chance to make it worse."

"So what? People will talk anyway."

"Let's git rid o' the thing. Nobody else knows about it. You and Marcel are both Galvanized Yanks so you ain't likely to talk. Me, I ain't anxious to stir up trouble fer my friends."

"Thanks. But it's evidence. When I got out of that Rock Island prison by agreeing to fight Indians I didn't put in any conditions. If the Confederacy is actually trying to start an Indian war I'm as much against it as I was against the other one."

He swung to stare hard at the big Cajun. "What about you, Marcel? This will likely make things a bit more uncomfortable for us."

Ladou shook his head. "Hear plenty big mouth already. No matter." Then he added with a shrug. "Long way to Louisiana. Here we fight Injuns."

Sawdust slapped him on the back. "We're with ye, Cajun. I guess we understand each other."

"Let's go," Barry said shortly. "We'll try to take the Indian ponies along. If they're too much trouble we'll have to shoot them."

There was no further mention of the count-stick, even when they overtook the mail coach and tossed the blanket bundle in on top of the mail sacks. An hour later they made camp for the night, there being no relief stations yet established along the new route. Barry simply picked a spot that was screened from casual observation but yet would not be vulnerable to a sneak attack. It seemed likely that the afternoon's ambush had been one of those spur-of-the-moment affairs on the part of the Indians but there was no point in assuming too much. There might be other warriors in the vicinity who could be brought into action by the two survivors.

They did not mention the evidence to any of the others but when supper was over and the first guards posted for the evening Barry went across to where Hardhead Maginnis was propped against a tree with his hat down across his eyes.

"Something's sticking in my craw," he announced. "Your passenger got off a remark about secessionists in the army today. I wasn't sure whether he intended it for me or whether it was a general bit of snootiness. Did you tell him I was once in the Confederate army?"

"Nope. He already knew it. At Fort Halleck he musta asked a lot o' questions."

"About me?"

"Mebbe. I dunno fer sure. He was bellyachin' to me about havin' to depend on this gang of bandits as his guard. And he didn't much like the idea of a Galvanized Yankee wearin' them stripes on his sleeves."

Barry laughed shortly. "I'm afraid my fine lads don't have the best social reputations in the army. And that includes me, of course."

"Mebbe he'll feel better after seein' how ye handled that

business this afternoon. Anyhow he oughta."

"Thanks. Sawdust mostly calls the turns about right."

"Tell me about that ugly polecat," Maginnis said with obvious interest. "Nobody else but you ever says a good word fer him. They tell me he got called Sawdust because most of the time he's spread out on saloon floors. But ye're hintin' that he runs things fer ye."

"That's about right. Private Featherstone isn't what the military manuals describe as the perfect soldier. Around camp or in town he can cause more trouble than a gallon of free whiskey. It's different in the wilds. He traveled with Bridger when he was a boy and he still knows what he learned."

"How come he ain't the sergeant then?"

"He was. Lost his stripes after one of his saloon brawls. Now he's willing to let me wear the stripes and try to keep him out of trouble. We understand each other."

"Mebbe ye'd oughta explain to the fat feller. He's kinda worried about bein' out here with two Rebs, a drunken mountain man, an Austrian deserter and a horse thief."

"Let him worry. I had a hunch it was me he was worrying about. Somehow it seemed as though I ought to know him."

"All I know about him is that he's in some kind of tradin' business. Used to be along the Ohio River somewhere. Now he's plannin' to build up some trade out here when the war's over."

"Thanks," Barry told him, turning away. Now he had something to think about. It was too much of a coincidence to be shrugged off. Rossiter needed a lot more study.

The stout man kept to himself that evening so there was

no opportunity to sound him out. On the following day they made slow time along the winding valley of Sybille Creek, the trail ill-defined and the need for caution a thing that made men ride tense, grim, sometimes more than a little edgy. Barry found little time to think about the mysterious passenger who had so many possible connections with his own past.

By noon of the following day it was beginning to seem certain that the attackers of the previous afternoon had not really been a war party but had been what Barry and Sawdust guessed. The thought should have relieved everybody but it didn't. Somewhere in the lodges of the hostiles a couple of chiefs were going to get mighty angry at hearing about how a courier under their protection had been killed by white soldiers. They would certainly try to save face if there were any warriors within striking distance.

The mail detail reached the Chugwater at dusk, the way now clear and with scant prospect of real Indian danger between this final camp and Fort Laramie. During the day Barry had avoided the coach and its surly passenger but at supper Rossiter took it upon himself to open hostilities.

"I see you found a rebel blanket on one of the savages, Sergeant. It must make you feel real proud to know that your friends in Richmond have offered bounties for Federal scalps."

"I don't know that they have," Barry told him quietly. "And I don't believe it—not that I have any friends in Richmond."

Rossiter sneered. "I suppose you'll deny that the rebels have been inciting these Indian raids that have plagued the frontier this summer?"

"I won't deny it because I don't know anything about it. My job is fighting Indians, not asking them about their politics."

A derisive snort came from behind the beard. "I suppose you'd rather not know. For a man in your position it could be awkward."

Barry turned to look him squarely in the eyes. "Mister," he said gently but with more than a hint of iron in the tone. "If you've got any complaints about the way I'm running this detail you can complain to the commander when we reach Fort Laramie. If you're prying into my personal life I'll tell you right now that it's none of your damned business."

"You are insolent, Sergeant!"

"Of course. I intended to be. You can also report that to the commander."

Featherstone interrupted in his best nasal twang. "Don't fuss with the fat bastard, Sarge. Punch him in the nose."

"You stay out of this!"

"Sure, Sarge, only he kinda makes me think about how ole Jim Bridger useta claim that the biggest mouths was always hitched up to the smallest minds. This fat sonofabitch is sure a . . ."

"I'll report the pair of you!" Rossiter stormed. "You'll find out . . ."

"We been reported before," Ben Samuels cut in. "So what happens? They can't throw us in the guard house because they need us fer all the dirty chores we always git—like playin' nurse maid to loud-mouth fat slobs." He winked at Barry as though reminding him that he had allies.

Rossiter almost choked on his supper but seemed to know that he was outnumbered. The rest of the meal went by with no more talk on that subject, Rossiter saying nothing at all. He was the first to finish, taking his blankets to the spot where he proposed to spend the night even before Sawdust and Samuels went out to relieve the pair who had been standing guard during supper.

After a while Maginnis looked across at Barry and remarked, "Seems like our passenger has kinda got it in fer ye, Sarge. Any idea why?"

Barry was still bothered by the feeling that he must have met Rossiter earlier but he shook his head. "Just one of those things, Hardhead. From his talk I'd say he comes from the same part of Tennessee that I did. Feeling ran pretty strong along the border when the war broke out and maybe he still feels it."

"Funny thing about that," Maginnis commented. "Seems like it's easier to hate a neighbor who don't agree with you than it is to hate a complete stranger."

Barry laughed. "You're almost as much of a philosopher as Sawdust. The only difference is that you don't claim to be quoting from Jim Bridger."

"Ye mean he makes them things up out of his own head?"

"Of course. Private Featherstone is quite a fellow. He's a little ashamed of having brains so he blames all his bright ideas on Bridger."

"You'd better git him primed to spring some real smart ideas on yer officers at the fort. Sure as hell this Rossiter pest is goin' to raise the roof when he gits a chance to talk to somebody with shoulder straps."

Barry shrugged. "If it wasn't Rossiter it would be some-body else. There's plenty of men in uniform who don't like the idea of a Galvanized Yankee wearing chevrons. I'm used to it."

CHAPTER 3

There was shell ice in the creek shallows when the little company moved out at dawn, all of them glad to be moving after a night in which the temperature had dropped sharply. They shivered but at the same time they felt pretty good about it. Indians generally stopped most of their raiding when cold weather arrived.

Barry rode out ahead with Sawdust until the trail led out of the hills. Then, having seen no sign of Indian trouble, he eased back to make his usual check on the other men. Ben Samuels seemed more than a little disturbed but his first words indicated that he was not worried over hostile Indians.

"I reckon I shot off my mouth too much last night, Sarge. That fat wampus kinda riled me. Mebbe he'll make trouble. Fer you, I mean."

"No matter."

"Fer me—no. It's like I told him; I ain't got nothin' to lose. But they could rip them stripes offa yer sleeves."

"Forget it. I'm hoping I'll lose these stripes anyway. Cap-tain Pritchard has been doing some writing for me. Maybe I'll be out of the army when we reach the fort."

The broad, homely face twisted into a frown. "Goin' to leave us? How come? Anyhow I didn't think you Galvies could get discharged."

"Maybe I won't be. I'm just hoping. I guess you heard that Arkansas, Louisiana, and Tennessee were being taken back into the Union now that Federal troops have them under control. According to what we heard about President Lincoln's orders our people get to be citizens again as soon as they take an oath of allegiance. I'm from Tennessee and I've already sworn allegiance in joining the army. That ought to make me a citizen."

"Likely it does. But do you have to run out on us? This here gang of hard cases ain't goin' to be the same without you." He grinned as he added, "Nobody else is goin' to admire havin' us around."

"Maybe the whole thing will be over shortly. It can't last long. In my case I'd like to get back to Tennessee. There's a lot of business matters that have needed attention ever since my father died two years ago. Maybe it's too late for me to save anything out of the wreck but I'd like to try. Captain Pritchard understands my situation and has been trying to arrange a parole or something for me."

Barry wondered why he was confiding in this fellow Samuels. He knew perfectly well that the man had evaded a prison term for horse stealing by joining an Ohio Cavalry regiment that was then sent to the frontier when the first emergency broke. Not many of the Eleventh Ohio Volunteer Cavalry still remained at Fort Laramie but Samuels didn't dare go home.

"Seems funny to think of you bein' anything but a soldier," the big man muttered. "You been out here as long as I can remember."

"I shouldn't have been a soldier in the first place," Barry replied, still a little amazed at himself that he should now have the urge to talk about a subject he had kept to himself so long. "Certainly not a Confederate soldier. I didn't believe in slavery and I felt that secession was a mistake. I just happened to get in."

"The draft?"

"No. Stupid choice. I'd been working in my father's freighting business which was mostly along the Ohio River and some of its feeders. We had a feeling that the big opportunities coming up would be in western trade so I came out here to look around. I liked what I saw but when I got home again the secession trouble was coming to a head. I'd been a lieutenant in our local militia company and they seemed to expect that I'd stay with it even though I'd been away from town for almost a year." He laughed without mirth as he explained, "If I hadn't kept the job they'd likely have elected a wealthy hot-head that I didn't like. That's what put me in the Confederate army. Petty dislike of another man."

"Anyhow you didn't stay there long," Samuels told him with a broad grin. "You was always a Galvanized Yank as far back as I remember."

"Sure. Fine war record I had! In September of sixty-one our company was mustered in as part of Tennessee Infantry. Right after Christmas we got orders to move into Fort Donelson. In February of sixty-two Grant took us out as prisoners. After that it didn't take me long to decide that I'd rather fight Indians than prison guards. I wanted to get back here to the west anyhow. So I became one of the first Galvanized Yankees—which is how it happened I've been around long enough to wear chevrons."

"We git into things in damned funny ways," Samuels

agreed. "You already know about me, I suppose."

Barry decided that the exchange of confidences had gone far enough. He'd gotten it out of his system. Now he didn't want to talk about it any more. "I've heard," he said dryly. "Keep your eyes open back here. We're closing in on the fort but there's no telling how bold the hostiles might get." Then he spurred his horse ahead, a little amazed at himself for having chosen an unrepentant horse thief as a confidante.

The mid-day sun had driven away the night chill when the coach rolled into Fort Laramie unchallenged and with only sight of a single mounted picket to suggest that the post maintained any vigilance at all. Barry knew why. Major Wood's entire command consisted of ninety men, most of them untrained militia or former Confederate prisoners. After the first year of the war there had been practically no regular troops in any of the western forts so each commander had to carry on his difficult task with whatever men he could get. Barry's guard unit—generally referred to as a squad in spite of its small size—was rated as one of the best outfits. Their varied backgrounds were no worse than the usual run and their record was something even a gang of outcasts could brag about. Which they did. Loudly.

Today the post showed its usual mixture of shabbiness and pomp. Two officers in dress uniforms and white gloves stood in the doorway of the adjutant's office, watching the arrival of the mail coach and its escort, while at one of the warehouses men on fatigue detail loaded a wagon. Every man in the detail wore a bandage of some sort. Laramie was garrisoned by its walking wounded, all able bodied men being on some sort of guard duty along the extended lines the fort was supposed to protect. It had been bad enough to guard the Mormon and Oregon Trails with their established relief posts, the six hundred miles of trail and telegraph lines from South Pass east to Julesburg straining everyone to the limit. Now with new routes along Lodgepole Creek and through the Laramie mountains the situation was even worse. There simply were not enough men to do the work. The best men could not have done it properly.

The fort itself showed the result of this shortage of manpower. Men able to do full duty remained on the post only long enough for scant rest and new orders. Routine work details had to be skipped. Buildings needed repair. The parade ground was high with grass and weeds in spite of the practice of letting horses graze there. More weeds choked walkways. A piece of the railing on the outside stairway of the commander's quarters had broken away and dangled untended. Fort Laramie would have been easy picking for any determined Indian attack but somehow the savages had never quite nerved themselves to the attempt even after succeeding in a daylight raid that swept a number of cavalry horses off the parade ground.

Barry saw to it that his squad rode in formation as they entered the post ahead of the coach. The men liked it that way. They were proud of their record in guarding mail coaches, proud of being condemned as the worst gang of thugs in the garrison. Lately they had also taken a perverse pride in showing critical officers that they could put on a good military show. Of course it was difficult for a ragged fellow like Private Featherstone to look spruce and proper but somehow he kept himself reasonably erect and maintained his place in the formation. Gerhardt Strauss took care of that. The Austrian had quite a gift for such things.

Barry halted them in front of the two white gloved officers, dismissing them with a crisp order after his salute had been returned. There was no need to issue any instructions. They would take care of their horses first and then start badgering the cook for decent food. After that he could only guess. Sometimes they didn't get into too much trouble before they could be sent out on the trail again.

He was glad to see that Adjutant Pritchard was one of the two men in the doorway. Captain Pritchard was the stabilizing influence in the garrison. With militia officers coming and going he was the man who had been carrying the real burden ever since being sent west. Wounded at Shiloh he had spent some months in a hospital and had then been assigned to the west as a semi-invalid. Now he was doing more than a well man's share. He was the man who had put the stripes on Barry's sleeves, the man who had showed himself a friend to the former prisoner-of-war.

An orderly with his left arm in a sling came around the corner to take position behind the officers as they stepped forward. Barry dismounted and turned his horse over to Samuels. Then he stepped forward two paces and announced, "Mail coach coming in, sir. No casualties although we were ambushed by hostiles along Sybille Creek." Almost as an afterthought he added, "One passenger on the mail coach. A Mr. Herbert Rossiter from Salt Lake City."

"Very good, Sergeant," Captain Pritchard said formally. "Lieutenant Addison, will you be so kind as to meet the passenger and escort him over to Old Bedlam? Make him as comfortable as possible."

The stern young lieutenant saluted and swung on his heel, something like disappointment showing in his eyes. Barry suppressed a grin. He knew well enough that Lieutenant Addison didn't approve of Galvanized Yankees who made good records. Addison would probably be well pleased to have this particular guard detail make some kind of blunder.

Pritchard motioned for Barry to follow him into the office. "Let's hear your complete report, Sergeant," he said loudly enough for Lieutenant Addison to hear. "How did you find the new trail?"

"Rough, sir. It will need some fixing if we're going to use it for any length of time."

"What about the Indians? Have they moved into the mountains in any strength?"

"I don't believe so, sir. The party that jumped us was a funny lot. We saw no other Indian sign. Anyway it's getting late in the season for big raids. They'll be hunting their winter camps before long."

"Let's hope so. But what about the party you fought? Sioux or Cheyenne?"

"Both, sir. And one Delaware. That's what made me say it was a funny lot. We killed four of the six, including the Delaware. He was carrying what Private Featherstone says is a count-stick. We think he was some sort of messenger taking a census of the tribes. He also carried a Confederate musket, cartridge box and blanket."

"You brought those things in?" Pritchard demanded quickly.

"They're with the mail sacks, sir."

"Get them. I'll have to rout out the commander for this. He's been sick again but I want him to hear about it."

Barry saluted and went out just as the coach was unloading its passenger. Rossiter eyed him dourly but did not speak so Barry paid no attention to him, simply reaching in and pulling out the blanket wrapped bundle and the Enfield musket. Behind him he heard the fat man announce loudly to Lieutenant Addison, "Evidence there. The rumors about rebel agents among the Indians has not been exaggerated. I suggest that your commander place every former rebel under strict guard until this crisis is over."

Barry turned in time to see the Lieutenant's puzzled frown but he made no comment. Loose talk wasn't going to be any help now.

Rossiter didn't seem to agree with that idea. He was blustering furiously about army stupidity in forcing a Denver passenger to come as far north as Fort Laramie. This time Barry didn't mind hearing the noise. The fat man wasn't making himself popular with that kind of talk and it was not going to earn him a better hearing if he should try to lodge complaints against the men of the guard detail.

Captain Pritchard was still alone in the bare little office when Barry took the bundle in and dumped it on the floor. "Smells pretty ripe, sir," he commented. "Likely full of fleas too."

The adjutant smiled crookedly. "It won't make half the stink that your report is going to stir up. If you're right, that is."

"I can imagine, sir. And I think you'll find this is what I told you."

This time the adjutant's smile broadened. "On the authority of no less a personage than Private Featherstone, I suppose?"

"Yes, sir."

"I don't know anybody more likely to have the right of it. Perhaps you don't know that we've had quite a bit of information on this possible Indian plot. Since you were on the post last, I mean."

"Real evidence, sir?"

"It seems so." He went to the door as though to assure himself that he still had some time before the commander's expected arrival. "You know about how much talk there was about Indian danger after Van Dorn used savages against Federal troops at the Battle of Pea Ridge. You must also be aware of the scare talk that went the rounds when Albert Pike was representing the Confederacy among the southwestern tribes. We're reasonably certain now that Pike was simply trying to keep the tribes peaceful so they wouldn't raid the Texas borders but plenty of southern sympathizers were willing to twist his efforts into Indian attacks on loyal settlements."

Barry nodded, aware that Pritchard was making this a rather personal affair. He wasn't speaking to a Galvanized Yankee but to a man he trusted, a man who could have no sympathy for any kind of attempt to stir up an Indian war.

"This time the Confederate government is using Indians as agents," Pritchard went on. "They've had a Creek named Tuk-a-Ba-Tche-Miko—or something like that—traveling among the Osages, Pawnees, Kiowas, Arapahos and God knows how many other tribes. There's a strong hint that he's undermining Bent's peace influence with the

Southern Cheyennes and we know that he uses count-sticks of some sort to send back his reports on the tribes he visits and their probable disposition."

"Sounds bad," Barry agreed. "I suppose our Delaware could have been working for him among the Sioux and Northern Cheyennes. Is there any hint as to exactly what he's trying to do?"

"I'd say that the recent Cheyenne depredations are hint enough. They've never let up since the August attacks. Denver is cut off again from the east. Our telegraph wire goes out about once a week. Right now we're running it blind. Haven't had a wire to Julesburg in six days. We don't really know how bad things are to the east and south."

He broke off as a stoop-shouldered man in a bathrobe came in. Major Woods waved aside the crisp salutes, a wan smile coming to his drawn features. "No formalities when I'm in this garb. Just get on with the story." After two years at Fort Laramie trying to do an impossible job he didn't need a bout with fever to make him look ill. He took the chair that Barry handed across to him, staring down at the articles on the floor.

"Your story, Sergeant," Pritchard prompted. "Tell it your own way."

Barry went through it quickly, omitting all details which had no bearing on the possible meaning of the evidence. Major Woods broke in twice with sharp questions but when it was over he forced a thin smile.

"You didn't help yourself much when you brought this stuff in, Sergeant. Why didn't you get rid of it?"

He waved off any possible answer and went on hastily, "Don't bother to reply. I'm not questioning your loyalty. I was only thinking that this is going to make it all the more awkward for us to keep you doing the work you've done so well. I mean that, Sergeant."

"Thank you, sir."

"Don't thank me. Captain Pritchard's the one who decided that we had a Galvanized Yank who knew his business and could be trusted. The point is that some people don't agree with us. We'll hear some loud noises about depending on a man who once served the politicians who are trying to get us all massacred."

He stood up shakily, still trying to force a smile. "It's your problem, Captain. I'm going back to bed before the surgeon catches me. I'll back you."

They watched his departure but then Pritchard growled, "I wonder what he thinks I'm going to do that'll need backing? Right now we can't even keep the mails going. While the telegraph is out we're not making any kind of move. We'll be lucky if we don't have to stand off half the Cheyenne nation with the handful of men we've got in the fort."

"As bad as that, sir?"

"Maybe not. I'm being gloomy because I simply don't know. We're cut off. That's bad enough."

CHAPTER 4

There was an interval of silence before Barry asked, "Anything on that problem of mine, Captain?" He had hesitated to bring it up while the worried adjutant had so much on his mind. Still he wanted to know.

Pritchard looked blank for a moment, then made an

impatient gesture. "Sorry, Sergeant. I forgot that you had your own troubles. Do you know a Mrs. Jesse Conway?"

Barry made no effort to hide his astonishment. "Mrs. Conway? What in . . . ?"

Pritchard's crooked smile made his whiskers look just a little more bristly than normal. "I was hoping you could explain. Last week we received a formal request that your grave should be properly marked and the bill sent to her."

"My grave! I don't understand that at all!"

"Nor does anyone else. May I ask who Mrs. Jesse Conway is?"

Barry shook his head, trying to get his thoughts together. "Her husband was to be my father's partner in that western venture I once told you about. Family friends for a long time and all that sort of thing." He did not think it important to mention that he had once expected Mrs. Conway to become his mother-in-law. "How did she ever get the idea that I needed a grave marker?"

"I don't know. The whole thing is muddled up by the fact that the letter was delivered something over a year late. I gather that it was found in the rubble of a burned out stage station and sent on with other mail that could still be deciphered. She wrote it in July of sixty-three. No details. Only the request and the offer to pay the bill."

When Barry made no comment he went on quickly, "I've been thinking of what this will do to those business affairs of yours but I can't offer you a bit of hope. Nobody is getting relieved while this crisis continues, your situation as a former prisoner only making the chances less. Nor do I have any information to give you. My correspondent at the Cairo supply base wrote that he would look into the affair but since then we've had very little mail. The raids along the Platte have virtually isolated us."

"Then it's still bad?"

"Very. At least two hundred people have died along the Platte trails. Women have been carried away, ranches burned out. And it's still going on."

"I understand, sir." Barry knew that there was no point in continuing the discussion so he asked quietly, "Shall I leave this stuff here on the floor?"

Pritchard nodded his understanding. "For a while anyhow. Get yourself some rest and a decent meal. No telling how soon you'll be riding again."

Barry headed straight for the barracks, certain that his men would have taken care of the stable chores promptly. That was one of the things they always did well. He found them swapping insults and stories with a similar squad that had just come in from an escort job down the North Platte. A brawny corporal named Wirtz was in charge, the rest of the crew being almost as mixed a lot as his own. A couple of Texas boys not out of their teens made up the Galvanized Yankee part of the group, the other pair being former militiamen, one from the Eleventh Ohio and the other a Kansan who had hated southerners since the days when he had fought them in the border troubles around Lawrence and Leavenworth.

"Purty quiet trip," Wirtz declared. "Seems like the Sioux are waitin' around to see if the Cheyennes are goin' to make a real war of it." Then he went on with an open sneer at Barry, "Seems like they must be gittin' ready to do that very thing—prodded along by the dirty rebels."

"Ain't got to the Sioux yet," Private O'Connell, the

Kansan, broke in. He always seemed to be Wirtz's echo in the feuds that had split this particular detachment. "Makes a man feel downright squeamish to have a couple o' Goddam rebels in the squad. Keep thinkin' they might start gittin' ideas about collectin' bounty money on my hair. If they'll buy scalps they'll take 'em!"

He had to shout to make himself heard with the final statement. Both of the Texas boys were on their feet, blistering O'Connell in profane unison. When Wirtz moved to defend him they brought him under attack also. Their appraisal of his person, habits, intelligence, and ancestry was pretty lurid but Wirtz didn't seem to mind. He let them run out of breath and then observed, "Rather have ye blackguardin' me to my face than puttin' a knife in my back. Not that it couldn't happen the other way."

That set them off again. Barry watched with some curiosity, having a feeling that Wirtz had deliberately stirred up this scene. He knew little about the man except what Samuels had said about him. Ben had known him in Eleventh Ohio and didn't think much of him. It was pretty clear that his present command hated him—with the exception of O'Connell.

There had been talk a year earlier when Wirtz had ordered a rash counter attack against some hostiles harassing a stagecoach. Two of his men had been killed in the fight but the Indians had fled, leaving him to bring the coach in safely. It was officially considered that he had done right in taking the offensive but the enlisted men who had seen comrades sacrificed didn't go along with the official opinion. The two Texas boys, Brady and Welland, were replacements for the dead men. Until that time Wirtz had avoided having captured confederates in his squad.

Barry decided that he might as well tell the men what he knew about the Delaware runner. It would leak out anyway so he might as well tell it straight. "Simmer down, boys," he told the angry Texans. "He's only trying to stir you up. Anyway you'll hear a lot worse before long. We just brought in some real evidence that there is a plot of some kind afoot. I didn't believe the gossip at first but now . . ."

"No Texans in it!" Welland snapped. "We been fightin' Injuns longer'n anybody else."

"Likely you're right. Anyhow, here's what it shapes up to be now." He explained what they had found on the Delaware, going on to pass along Captain Pritchard's appraisal of the present situation. "The new post this side of Julesburg still hasn't been completed and they're having trouble getting supplies and materials to it. All of us know that Colorado militia hit a couple of Indian villages this spring. Either of those things might put the Cheyennes on the war path. Nobody can be sure that they're being stirred up to war. This could be an attempt like the first one, simply to keep the Indians peaceful where the Confederacy is concerned."

"Ye make it sound real good," Wirtz sneered. "Bein' a Reb ye'd have to."

"Corporal, I'll tell you something, even if it isn't any of your damned business. I wasn't in favor of the Confederacy in the first place. At this stage I think the southern people are being betrayed by stubborn idiots. The war is over. They just won't stop fighting and recognize that they're licked."

Wirtz started to make another scoffing remark but Barry

cut him off. "Now that I'm started let me finish. If you want to believe me you can. If you don't—you can go to hell. I figure it this way. Grant's hammering what's left of Lee's army in Virginia. Sheridan has wrecked the Shenandoah Valley. The west is knocked out, Sherman is well down through Georgia. Lincoln has been re-elected over a candidate who might have given the Confederacy easy terms. There's not a port left open to the South and three seceded states are already back in the Union. Confederate money is no good, which means that the southern people have admitted that they know their government will never pay off. It's only a few stubborn fools who won't surrender and stop the killing."

"Nice speech," Wirtz growled. "But ye're fergettin' somethin'. Them same fools what won't admit they're licked would be jest the kind o' hairpins to take out their spite by startin' a Injun war."

There was no opportunity for the talk to go on. The crippled orderly came to the barracks door and yelled, "Cap'n Pritchard wants to see you, Sarge. Bring Sawdust with you—on the double."

Barry grinned at Samuels. "I'm guessing that our friend Rossiter has made his complaint. I wonder how come you didn't get called in?"

"Want me to go along? I'll tell the bastard to his fat face."

"Whoa! No use hunting trouble. Anyway you didn't get called. It could be something else."

It was. Pritchard told them quickly that the telegraph wire had started working shortly after Barry went to the barracks. It had brought troubling news. Not only was the raiding getting worse all along the South Platte but a train of ten wagons had left Julesburg just after the wire was cut and no one had seen them since. The Colorado militia on patrol in the neighborhood of old Fort Lupton was on the lookout for them but as yet had not found them.

"That part we'd had a hint on," Pritchard told them soberly. "Our wire to Denver has been working most of the time. But we thought that the wagons had halted at the new post they're calling Fort Sedgwick."

"Then they've had ample time to get through?"

"I think so. This wagon outfit was a late starter to begin with and they were held up on military orders twice when the August raids got so bad. We heard that they were at Julesburg waiting for an escort to see them through." He let a wry smile pull his beard out of line. "That escort was to have been our reinforcements so I guess we were wishing instead of thinking. Anyway no troops arrived."

"You mean that the wagons were coming here?"

"No. To Denver. The town's anxious enough for them to get through, of course. Six or seven wagon loads of flour and salt pork can mean a lot to people who've been cut off most of the summer. And a nice price for the freighters too. Our men were to have taken them along to where the Colorado militia could pick them up. Then the escort would come on north to Fort Laramie."

"But it didn't work out that way?"

"Not at all. They passed right through Sedgwick, taking the risk of unguarded travel. Our scouts know that they crossed the South Platte and left the regular trail. We don't know why and our patrols didn't dare trail them beyond the point where they crossed. They're lost, sure as hell! If they're not all dead."

"Sounds bad. Are we expected to do something about it?"

"They always expect us to do something. You might think we had a full army corps out here! My idea was that maybe you and Sawdust might make a search for them. If they're already dead, get back the best way you can. If they're simply lost, try to get them through to where the Colorado boys can take over."

Barry realized that the use of the nickname was intended to tell him that this was a completely informal discussion. "It's a long trip down there," he said shortly. "Why can't the Colorado militia make the search?"

"They're worse off for men than we are right now. Major Chivington has taken his whole regiment down toward the Arkansas somewhere, scheming up some kind of an attack on the hostile villages, I believe. North of Denver they don't have enough men on hand for decent guard duty."

"What about it, Sawdust?" Barry asked, turning to the lanky scout. "You know the country a lot better than I do. Could we find 'em?"

"Mebbe. Like ole Jim Bridger useta say, 'A man can't never tell 'til he tries—and then sometimes he gits kilt tryin'.'"

"I won't order you on this patrol," Pritchard said soberly. "If you go you're going as volunteers."

"I'm game," Barry told him. "I might as well fight Indians as other soldiers. And that's what is going to happen if I have to listen to much more of that talk about damned rebels buying scalps!"

"Then get ready. Put your gear together and get some sleep. I think you ought to slip away from here during the night. We're watched all the time."

They were on their way out when Barry asked, "Did the telegraph come up with anything on this possible plot, Captain?"

"Not a thing. We've had some interruptions since the wire started working again so our messages haven't been too coherent. By the way, don't fret too much over having to leave that previous gang of cut-throats you call a squad. We've got orders to halt all mail coaches until the emergency is over. No guard details will be going out. We'll need them right here."

Barry caught the officer's grin and waved a hand. He didn't mind a man like Pritchard calling his men names. Pritchard knew that they had been doing their job well.

It took a little time to get preparations made but then he turned the rest of the chore over to Strauss and Ladou so that he and Featherstone could try for some sleep. There was no telling when they'd get another chance for a few hours of uninterrupted rest.

It was Ladou who woke him. The barracks had lights burning in it and every man in sight was getting into his uniform, most of them grumbling but still making progress. Barry had time to note that Corporal Wirtz and his squad were dressing along with the others and then Ladou explained, "We go find the wagons. Everybody."

"New orders," Samuels told him from across the big bare room. "Somebody has been throwin' weight around. Commander's sendin' every man he kin spare. Lieutenant Addison's goin' along."

Barry brushed the sleep away, groping for an explanation. Major Woods was taking quite a chance in sending away the only able bodied men on the post. Of course, they would have been on guard detail along the trails anyway so perhaps it was a calculated risk. Other squads would be coming in as the general halt was called on mail movements.

"Cap'n wants to see you when you get awake," Ladou told him. "You got orders?"

"The usual thing. Wear overcoats and take extra blankets. Two canteens and plenty of hard rations. I'll tell you more when I've found out what this is all about."

Five minutes later he was in the adjutant's office once more. This time the grim faced Lieutenant Addison was also on hand. Barry had managed to keep clear of Addison during the time they had been on duty at Laramie but he was under no illusions about the man. Addison was a Kansan like O'Connell. He hated secessionists but he hated the slave interests worse. Barry had often wondered if the young man had worked with old John Brown in the troubled days before the big war but it had never seemed smart to ask any questions.

Pritchard nodded for him to take a seat, pointedly ignoring Addison's clear disapproval. "Quite a lot of things have been happening, Sergeant. One is a message about your personal affairs. I'll get that out of the way first. It seems that your business back east got badly tangled up because you were reported dead. I've asked for an investigation but I'm not sure what it means. Naturally they don't put much of that sort of thing on the wire when so much else demands attention. Lucky I had a friend in the right place or we wouldn't know that much."

Barry did not reply. There was nothing to say. He tried to

brush the confusion away as Pritchard went on with the matter of change of plans.

"Major Woods had a message from Department Headquarters. We are asked to give every possible assistance to one Herbert Rossiter who seems to be a pretty important fellow back in the states. He's out here to establish a freighting business and the reason he has been so anxious to reach Denver is that he wants to be there to meet some wagons that are coming out with supplies that should bring high prices."

Barry stared. "Don't tell me that . . ."

"Exactly. Julesburg confirms that the lost wagons are commanded by a fellow named Shingle. Rossiter asked us to inquire. Shingle is his employee. The upshot of it all is that Major Woods has decided to send as strong a force as possible. Your men and those of Corporal Wirtz make up the detachment. Lieutenant Addison is in command."

There was a moment of silence in which Barry tried to guess what was being left unsaid. Then the adjutant took the bull by the horns. "There's another point. Our orders are to place no captured Confederates in any position of trust until we know what this reported plot means. Major Woods has assigned Lieutenant Addison for reasons you must understand. My orders to the Lieutenant are to use your skill and Featherstone's as much as possible. Officially you are not to be trusted; personally I think you know how I feel."

"I'd better rip off the stripes, sir," Barry said evenly. "I can scout as a private as well as Sawdust can."

"No. This is going to blow over. I don't want it on your record. If we're to have any chance at getting you back home it'll be because you've done good service. I'm sure Lieutenant Addison understands."

Barry wasn't so sure. He didn't figure that Addison was an understanding sort of man.

"You'll leave in about an hour," Pritchard told him. "I'll want to inspect weapons and equipment before you ride out. Now get along and see to it that everything's right for a hard trip."

Addison went along with him. Out in the chill of the night the lieutenant said flatly, "I'll undertake to accept your suggestion, ex-Sergeant Barry. As of now you can consider yourself as a private soldier for purposes of this detail. I'm quite in agreement with those who don't believe rebels should be trusted."

"Thank you, sir," Barry told him formally, keeping his voice from showing the feeling that was behind it. "No authority, no responsibility. That suits me fine, sir."

Captain Pritchard appeared on the parade ground as the detail prepared to ride. He made a brief speech to the men, telling them what they were supposed to do and why they might expect to find difficulties. "Those wagons must be somewhere in a big triangle of rocky country between the two branches of the Platte and west of the Denver telegraph line. I can't tell you how to find them and neither can Lieutenant Addison. You'll just have to search."

He turned to aim a question at Sawdust. "Private Featherstone, you know that country better than anyone else. Is there any reasonable route by which wagons could move through the country on the north side of the South Platte?"

"Nothing good, Cap'n. They coulda swung up Pawnee Crick if'n they made their crossin' soon enough. Next likely place would be Wildcat Crick."

"Are there trails along either stream?"

"Not real trails, Cap'n. Most folks don't go through there at all. When the army quit usin' Lodgepole and switched to the Cherokee Trail they didn't leave the South Platte fer a lot more miles. Nobody else goes through on the north side. Plumb wild country."

"What about Pawnee Creek? It could be used, I understand. Can you find its headwaters from here?"

Sawdust grinned. "Cap'n, I kin find the dry washes that feed into it. Won't be no headwaters at this time o' year. Wagons likely would be along Wild Horse Fork—if'n the Injuns ain't wiped 'em out yet. It's the only fork likely to have water—and they'll sure as hell be needin' some."

"So you know the country. Good. You're the guide." He lowered his voice to add, "I'm depending on you and Sergeant Barry."

There didn't seem to be any reason to say more. Captain Pritchard had been pretty frank in the past and Barry had met his frankness. Both of them knew that there would be problems, the same kind of problems Barry had been weathering for almost three years. Pritchard was simply asking for a continuation of patience.

CHAPTER 5

There was an interruption then as Addison began to make his final inspection. He found two things about which he made complaints. One was that there were three more horses than men. The other was that four of the men were failing to carry regulation cooking kits.

"My fault, sir," Barry spoke up. "I passed the word to my boys that this would be a forced march in bad country. They knew what I meant. Extra horses, extra canteens, hard rations, and no extra hardware."

"That sounds proper to me," Pritchard cut in. "Lieutenant, you'd better see to it that the rest of the men in your detachment adopt the same equipment. Use the spare horses to carry extra ammunition."

Addison barked orders at Wirtz, then turned and went away across the parade ground in the darkness. Barry was close enough to the adjutant so that he could make a low-voiced comment. "I'm afraid Mister Addison won't feel any better about me than he did before."

"Hmmph!" Pritchard did not try to conceal his ill humor. "Addison is an ass. Raw militiaman trying to put on all of the trappings of the regular service when he doesn't know how to handle the first fundamentals of his job! You should see the paper he filed with me a few minutes ago!"

Barry could guess from the Captain's tone. "Formal protest of his orders, you mean?"

"Exactly. Worded like a criminal indictment. He states that he can assume no responsibility for results when he is compelled to take with him several soldiers of dubious loyalty and one civilian whose interests may run counter to military necessity. That's the simplified version, at least."

"You mean Rossiter is going with us, sir?"

"He insists—and our orders are to give him what he wants. I might add that he protested having you on the patrol. You know why, of course."

"I'm a bit surprised. He doesn't like me—and probably he's afraid of all former Confederates—but he certainly

49

knows that I can fight Indians. A smart businessman wouldn't let prejudices interfere with doing the right thing."

"He was pretty violent about it but he's still a civilian and I'll be damned if I take orders from him. Now let me put in a piece of better information. One of my friends slipped in a personal message on the wire. Your father's claims against the government were settled in cash. I don't know when, how or anything. Just that."

Barry smiled in the darkness. "That's some help. With the Conways asking questions about me I can guess that they'll be taking care of whatever they can."

"Lucky I could tell you something good. Maybe it'll help to keep your mind off the wrangling that'll make this job a nuisance. Every time you feel like kicking Addison or spitting in Rossiter's eye just tell yourself that maybe things are going to work out."

Barry laughed. "Sure."

Ten minutes later the little column moved through the chilly darkness toward the ford of the Laramie River. Addison went out ahead with a mounted picket to lead the column across. He had given only brief orders for the march but it was noteworthy that he had put Barry and Samuels at the rear with the extra horses. Across the river he maintained the same alignment, following the well marked Oregon Trail. It seemed clear that while the command followed the North Platte he did not propose to depend on any guides. For the first few miles, at least, he could establish his authority by riding ahead. Barry grinned crookedly at the thought. Probably Addison didn't even guess that the men behind him understood what he was doing and were amused by it.

Once away from the tangled approaches to the ford they rode rapidly in the thin light of a waning moon, alternately riding and walking the horses. At least the commander knew that much about his business. One of the big risks in this whole enterprise—in addition to hostile Indians—was the danger of ruining horses.

It was a silent march, only the hoofbeats and the creak of leather or the jingle of equipment reminding men that they were not alone. Barry understood that most of them didn't want to talk. Wirtz's men were sulky at having been made to look bad in the matter of equipment. Barry's squad resented the treatment of their leader. All of them were uneasily aware of the way the stars were blotted out in the western half of the sky. Snow would make the job even worse than it now shaped up to be.

When they left the river at the mouth of Cherry Creek Addison issued new orders. "Privates Featherstone and Barry!" he snapped. "Scout ahead. Try to keep an interval of a quarter of a mile. The rest of you continue as before."

Barry could hear the angry murmurs around him as Addison addressed him as Private Barry but he silenced his men quickly. "Forget it. We'll have enough fighting without starting any among ourselves. And don't let anybody bait you into anything!" Then he rode out ahead with Sawdust, rather pointedly forgetting to salute the commander as he rode past. Addison would not miss the omission but there wasn't very much that he could do about it. A man who had just been demoted—but who is still needed—can't be subject to much more in the way of penalty.

When the first streaks of dawn began to redden the still clear eastern sky they were across Cherry Creek. By that time Sawdust couldn't keep his curiosity bottled up any longer. "Danged if I kin figger ye out, Sarge. That young jackanapes demotes ye right outa nothin' and ye don't even bust him in the eye. Not only that but ye've been grinnin' like a chessy-cat. What's goin' on anyhow?"

"Lieutenant Addison is taking me at my word. I offered to serve on this expedition as a private, being as how I'm not officially to be trusted. You'll notice he didn't get around to it until we were well clear of the fort."

He went on to explain the tangled relations involved and Sawdust nodded. "You and Cap'n Pritchard sure seem to git along good. Old friends?"

"Not exactly. We met a long time ago. He was on the invalid list after Shiloh. I was a prisoner. He drew limited duty at the prison. At the time we were both lieutenants and . . . somehow we seemed to understand each other."

"That still ain't enough to explain how come ye're so damned happy. Did ye git some good news about affairs back home?"

Barry motioned toward the dark pile of clouds in the west. "Could be we won't be getting any of that," he observed. "It doesn't seem any closer than it did during the night."

Sawdust snorted audibly. "So it's none o' my damned business. I'll shet up."

"I didn't mean that. I'm trying to keep myself from getting careless by having my thoughts somewhere else. You're entitled to know as much as anybody. More than most."

"Thanks. I ain't pryin'."

Barry laughed then, some of the tightness going out of him. It was funny to see a fellow like Sawdust putting on a show of injured dignity. But there was more than comedy involved. Sawdust had become a loyal friend. For no reason other than that Barry suddenly had the desire to tell him the whole story, even the parts that Captain Pritchard did not know.

"It was this way. My father had taken me into his freighting business, as I told you before, the idea being that we'd try to build up a western branch. Our main business was from the Ohio Valley into the Tennessee back country. We had steamboats on the Cumberland and the Tennessee. There were warehouses in Tennessee, Kentucky, and Illinois. We were planning to take on a new partner before venturing into the western trade, a man named Conway who did a lot of the wagon business that tied up with our steamboat trade."

"Sounds like a good deal," Featherstone commented. "And don't stop the yarn because ye see dust ahead. Them's buffler."

"There was another angle. Jess Conway had a daughter, a very pretty daughter. She and I were pretty good friends. We were planning to marry, and both families liked the idea. Everything was fine until I went back after my trip out here. Secession was splitting the partnership plans just as it was splitting the country. The Conways believed in the Union. You know how I happened to get on the other side. Linda and I argued it out and broke up. Then the Conways went up into Ohio, losing some of their property when the Confederacy seized it. After that I was playing soldier and didn't hear any more about them."

"Until now?"

"Right. Somehow they think I'm dead." He went on to tell what Pritchard had reported. "Affairs are in a mess but I think the Conways will do what they can. Of course, it won't be much if they think I'm dead."

"Great snakes!" Sawdust exclaimed. "I try to find out why you been a-grinnin' and now it don't seem like ye've got a damned thing to grin about."

"Maybe not. But it's good to know that Mrs. Conway still thinks enough of me to want my grave to be marked."

Sawdust laughed loudly. "A hell of a nice thought, I don't think! But mebbe ye've got a point. Better to have folks on yer side even if'n they don't know they're takin' care o' yer claims."

"But aggravating not to know where I stand."

"Like ole Jim Bridger useta say, 'What ye don't know won't hurt ye—and it gives other folks somethin' to laugh at.' If ye kin git happy over that kind of a deal go right ahead. Grin, dammit!"

"Maybe I will. The Conways are mighty decent folks. Once I was pretty happy to think that I was going to have in-laws that were the kind of folks they are. Maybe I just like to remember things like that."

"Also ye figger this gal might still be waitin'?"

"It's possible. I know a lot of time has passed and . . ."

He let it drift off without finishing it. More than three years had passed since he'd had his parting quarrel with Linda Conway. There would have been no reason for her to think about him again, no matter whether she believed him dead or alive. The realization was sobering. Now he wasn't so sure that he felt so happy about the prospect of re-establishing business claims.

The clouds had begun to move in by the time they reached Horse Creek. They found a little decent water there; Sawdust filled his canteens and rode on ahead while Barry remained to make a report and to see whether the little column would make a halt. It was nearly mid-day and they had covered a lot of miles since midnight.

Addison came up to meet him, his thin features showing no feeling as he asked, "Trouble?"

"No, sir. We thought you might be calling a rest halt here. By digging some holes the men can get fairly good water in the creek bed."

"Have you found any Indian sign?"

"Not a trace, sir. It's not country they'd likely be using."

"Very well. Get back to your post. We'll stop only long enough for water. And, Barry . . . the double canteen idea is a good one. The country is worse than I imagined."

Barry restrained his grin but saluted as he swung his horse away. A salute seemed like a reasonably good acceptance of what seemed like a small show of decency on the part of the Lieutenant. Maybe the fellow wasn't as bad as he made himself sound.

By following Horse Creek upstream they continued to set a good pace. The wind was freshening and the clouds blotted out all traces of blue sky so Barry was not surprised when Trooper Brady galloped forward to announce that Lieutenant Addison proposed to make an early camp. The scouts were to advise as to whether there was a suitable spot close ahead.

"The Goddam four-flusher won't admit it," the Texan

grinned, "but he's beat! So he's makin' out that he's callin' a halt because old pus-gut's wore out. Not that it ain't a good idee; the broncs can't hold up much longer."

Barry glanced questioningly at Sawdust but the scout only shrugged. "One place is as good as another. This lousy country's all alike. Tell him to pull up anywhere."

Brady nodded and went back to the column. That night there was little talk in camp. Men ate their hard rations, drank their coffee, took care of their horses and stood their guard duty without even bothering to grumble. They were too tired to waste words. Addison assigned guard details and fell asleep without eating. He didn't even know when it began to snow.

"Easy day tomorrow if the snow don't git too bad," Samuels muttered to Barry when they happened to see each other staring at the sleeping figures of both Addison and Rossiter. "The boy wonder is gonna be too saddle-sore to git real ornery. And the fat jasper is worse. Makes me feel awful sorry."

"Don't let it run away with you," Barry warned him dryly. "I don't like either of them any better than you do but we might need both of them before this is over."

The snow ended before midnight, the thin white layer on the ground offering no particular problem when they moved out in the cold gray dawn. Addison snapped out his orders almost as angrily as before. Rossiter glared at everybody. Normal bad humor seemed complete.

It was still early in the morning when they broke away from Horse Creek, Barry waiting at the turn-off to pass the word about refilling canteens. Now the column had to move into country where almost no trails existed between the now abandoned Cherokee and Lodgepole routes. Few emigrants had ever ventured into this wasteland of broken prairie, sand hills, and alkali washes. For a good two days they could not hope to find decent water. He explained the matter carefully to Lieutenant Addison and heard the young officer issue crisp orders about refills and not using water unless necessary.

"Better keep an eye on them, sir," he ventured. "The Cottonwood and Two Mile headwaters won't be any better than what we've been seeing. It could be more than two days, I'm afraid."

Rossiter picked that moment to break in. "Are you still taking advice from a rebel, Mister Addison? I thought you . . ."

"I didn't ask your opinion, sir!" Addison snapped. "We have scouts because they are supposed to know these things. Please do not interfere in military matters!"

Barry had no illusions. This was not any gesture toward himself but was merely an indication that Addison's intolerance was greater toward Rossiter. Still it seemed to rate some kind of acknowledgment so he saluted before riding away.

There were other brief conferences during the afternoon as they picked a way through the barren country. Addison maintained his aloof grimness but it was notable that he was coming to depend more and more on his scouts. Not once did he even mention the lost wagons, his entire concern being to see that the command found its way through the wilderness of sand and rock. And maybe that was smart enough. For all any of them knew this mission was already a waste of time and effort. The wagons—and their people—might have been destroyed by this time. Or they might have found their way through to safety. No one gave the latter possibility much thought. The whole idea was to hope that somewhere the wagoners were holding out and would continue to do so until help arrived. There was no time to be wasted but still they had to avoid the wrong kind of haste. Clearly, Addison was a fast learner.

Then they found Indian sign. Barry signaled for the column to hold up while he and Sawdust tried to work out a readable story. Nearly a hundred unshod ponies had left a north-south trail which intersected their own direction at a long angle. There were no travois marks so it evidently had been a war party of some kind.

"About a week old," Sawdust reported after a few minutes. "I'd say there was mebbe thirty warriors. The rest was spare ponies."

"Moving south or a little southwest. You think they might have been after those wagons?"

"Mebbe. If they knew about 'em. More likely a war party out huntin' fer any deviltry they could come across. Could be we'll find trouble even if'n we don't find any wagons."

They moved ahead, Barry dropping back to report. It was all too obvious that the Indian sign was adding to the grim tension that already gripped the detachment. Even when he stressed—rather loudly—the fact that the tracks were a week old the men didn't seem to ease very much. Nor did Addison.

There was an odd change in morale during the next day. Partly it was because the Indian sign did not appear again but mostly it was a matter of trail-hardened troopers holding up better than the two men they had begun to accept as their immediate enemies. As Addison and Rossiter began to suffer more acutely, the men in the ranks pushed harder, showing a positive enthusiasm for fast progress. Barry became aware of what was happening each time he dropped back to make reports but it wasn't until night that he knew how far it had gone. Then he went to Corporal Wirtz.

"You fellows are making it tough on the greenhorns, aren't you?" he asked in an undertone.

The big man grinned. "We don't make it that way. We just ain't grievin' none because it's so. But what do you care? You're gettin' as much of a dirty deal as anybody."

"It's your responsibility, Wirtz. I'm just a private so far as this job is concerned. If you let those men collapse you'll be the one that has to take care of them. So go easy."

"You got a point, Sarge." He laughed shortly as Barry stared. "I ain't so stupid. This is the kind of job you know how to do. I'm still seein' that third stripe on your arm."

"Thanks," Barry told him. "I guess we understand each other after all."

On the fourth day they found a fresher Indian trail which swung down out of the northeast to head between some broken hills and take a due south direction. When Barry reported it, Lieutenant Addison promptly called a halt and motioned for the whole detachment to move in.

"I'm not blind, men," he said without ceremony. "I know that we all depend on Sergeant Barry's judgment and I have the best respect for his experience. He tells me that the war party ahead of us may be Indian reinforcements going to aid whatever hostiles have already caught up with these lost wagons. I'm accepting his estimate and I want him to tell you what he thinks we ought to do."

Rossiter began to bluster weakly but Addison pulled himself up for one stern effort. "Shut your face!" he snarled. "This is not easy for me so don't make it worse. Tell them, Sergeant!"

"Yes, sir." Barry made it formal. This was no time to play up a small victory. From here on every man's firm cooperation was going to be vital. Discomfort was about to be replaced by a very real danger.

CHAPTER 6

"We've struck the trail of what looks like a war party of maybe twenty Cheyennes," Barry told his listeners. "We're guessing that somewhere to the south another party caught up with the wagons but couldn't handle them. This new outfit is joining the fight."

"A wild guess!" Rossiter snapped.

"Exactly. But it fits. We've got to hope it's that way. The other choice is worse, and I think you know what I mean. At any rate, we figure we've got to trail this gang of hostiles in hopes that they'll lead us to the wagons. That means we'll need to ride with skirmishers out. In this broken country an ambush would be mighty easy to lay."

"What about water?" Addison asked. "Any chance of finding it in this direction?"

"As much as any other, sir."

"How far are these Indians ahead of us?"

"Not more than a day, I believe. That's why we have to take the extra precautions."

"Very well. Assign the men as you see fit, Sergeant."

"Yes, sir." Again he kept it quietly formal. "Featherstone and I will continue to take the lead. O'Connell and Samuels are the rear guard. Ladou and Brady take the right flank, Strauss and Welland the left. All of you men know what's expected of you. Let's move out."

He cut off a question that Wirtz was about to fire at him. "Corporal, you'd better make it a point to keep an eye on the way the horses are holding up. Have the men change off on the spare animals a little more often. Also, you'd better start breaking in Mr. Rossiter as a horse holder just in case we need him. It could happen."

He swung closer to add in a lower voice, "I want your men to ride with mine for a while. Once they get the knack of handling the outrider job the way we've worked it out I think you'd better start breaking up those teams I just named."

"What the hell! Don't you think my men know how to ride flankers?"

"I want to make sure. Also I'd like to know just how they're doing it. If they pick up our pattern I won't need to worry about that part. All right with you?"

Wirtz shrugged. "You're callin' it, Sarge."

They moved on, following the Indian sign. At noon they halted for a rest and coffee; Barry quietly checked with his own men to see what they had to say about the other troopers who had been working with them. All of them seemed satisfied. Even Samuels had no complaint to offer about the way O'Connell was going along with the new arrangement.

In mid-afternoon they lost the sign. It was clear that they were moving into an area where the snow had been mixed with some rather heavy rain which had washed out the tracks entirely. It forced Barry to the opinion that the trail was older than they had guessed and it posed a problem of how to proceed with their plans. At the same time it settled one worry. The arroyos had water in them. It was muddy but neither the men nor the horses seemed to mind. After being on short water-rations they could swallow anything.

An hour later they were approaching a line of bluffs which Sawdust believed flanked the upper reaches of the Cottonwood. There had been no new Indian sign but this would be a dangerous area. Indians on the bluffs could easily spot the approach of the patrol. Accordingly Barry left Sawdust alone to keep watch and went back to propose a halt.

"It's a fair place to stop, Lieutenant," he explained. "The horses need all the rest they can get so a halt here will give them a breather while we look things over. If Sawdust and I can pick up that sign again we'll know what to do next. Maybe we'll have to make a move at night. Then we'll need all the energy the horses can work up."

"As you see fit, Sergeant. When do you expect to get back here?"

"It's likely to be an hour or so after sunset. You might look around here and pick one of these draws for a camping spot. Then you could keep a small fire that wouldn't show far to the south but would give us a way to find out."

Addison managed a tired grin. "You think of everything, Sergeant. Go right ahead."

Barry returned the grin and rode back to where Sawdust was waiting. The lanky man eyed him quizzically. "Still got Addison eatin' outa yer hand?"

Barry nodded. "I don't believe our unhappy Lieutenant is as stupid as we've been letting ourselves think. Once he got too tired to let his prejudices run his life he started using his head real good."

"Ole Jim Bridger useta have a sayin' about that. He claimed that most folks kept their prejudices because then they could always sound real serious and important without havin' the work and worry of doin' any thinkin'."

"Fine. Now did Jim Bridger tell you how to sneak up on a line of bare hills?"

Sawdust winked broadly. "Nothin' to it, Sarge. Stick close to the low spots and keep an eye on the high ones. Easy."

It wasn't exactly easy but the rest of the idea worked out well enough. Keeping to the shallow gulleys all the time, never crossing a barrier ridge unless they could get even higher ground in front of them, they worked forward slowly. It forced them to cover a good three miles to make a mile of progress but they still had daylight when they began the climb into the bluff country itself. There was no indication that they had been spotted or that any lookouts had been posted among the squatty crags.

Sawdust led the way through the maze of weathered buttes, seeming to grope a little but always working in the same southerly direction. Finally he held up his hand and led his horse behind a big chunk of the porous limestone which was the base of a ragged turret of yellow sand. "Looks like we hit plumb center, Sarge. Did ye see 'em?"

"Wagons or Indians?"

"Both. We'd better tie the broncs here fer a spell while

we git a good look."

Barry was surprised when he saw how close they had come to the tense little scene in the shallow valley beyond the buttes. The white-topped wagons in their close defense circle near the cottonwoods seemed almost within rifle range. He could make out the stock herded inside the enclosure but no humans moved anywhere. Evidently the wagoners were staying out of sight while they watched the antics of the war party which occupied a bit of high ground a quarter of a mile to the west. Except for the milling savages it was a quiet sort of scene but neither watcher liked that kind of quiet. Even at the distance they could see that two of the wagon tops showed the blackening of fire. And some of the stock in the emergency corral were down, probably dead as the result of an earlier attack.

"Still got ten wagons," Sawdust growled. "Mebbe they ain't such greenhorns as they sounded. They done real good to git this far."

"Close to forty hostiles," Barry said. "Looks like we made a good guess. About half of the Cheyennes have been keeping the wagons in a running fight while they waited for this other band to show up. I wonder why they don't attack?"

"Been makin' medicine. The first lot ain't been doin' so good. Now the other charmin' jolly-boys have showed up and they're goin' to crow a little at havin' to show the first lot how to do it. That's Injun fer ye. If'n the damned varmints didn't have to go through so much hocus-pocus in their fightin' they'd beat the hell out of our side every time."

"You think they'll hit the wagons tonight?"

"Nope. That ain't Injun nature either. They ain't in no hurry. Tonight they'll whoop it up and git theirselves all fired up fer countin' some coups in the mornin'. Likely they'll heave some lead into the wagons durin' the night jest to keep the folks edgy but there ain't goin' to be no big push before dawn. Then it'll come. Hard!"

Barry had seen and heard enough. He started to inch back toward the horses. "Let's get the rest of the boys. Maybe we can work something out."

Sawdust followed closely. "Jest so it ain't Addison what works it out. That polecat's goin' to be rested up a mite by the time we git back. Mebbe he'll start rememberin' that he's wearin' the fancy uniform."

"That's the risk we take when we get into the army. Come on."

When they found the bivouac in the gulley it was well past sundown, only the glow of the fire guiding them in after they had circled twice without spotting the place in the night. They found Addison asleep so they took time for what passed as a meal before awakening him. Then they awakened all of the men who were in the camp. One way or another the command would be making a move so everyone ought to know what was happening.

Barry explained what they had seen, even going out of his way to tell Rossiter that the train appeared to be reasonably intact except for the indication of some damage to wagon tops. "We couldn't tell anything about their casualties but it's likely they've suffered some. It's a sure thing they didn't fight their way this far without having things mighty hot—and I don't mean just the burning of canvas."

Addison was crisp and to the point. "What's our best

chance of getting to them, Sergeant?"

"It's hard to tell until we get the command back there and see what the hostiles have done since dark. If the Indians are where they were at dusk we might circle and come in on the wagons from the east. We might even get in unseen. Then we could surprise the Cheyennes when they make their strike at dawn. Our extra guns ought to give them quite a jolt."

"But you're not sure the Indians will hold their position?"

"No, sir."

"Then we'll decide later. Pass the word. We move out immediately."

Men hurried to saddle up and to pass the word to guards. Sawdust edged toward Barry as the pair of them changed their saddles to a couple of the extra horses. "Sounds like Junior's got his vinegar back. Now that he's had some sleep he could git real proddy."

"Let him," Barry muttered in reply. He was beginning to feel the continuing strain. There was no reason for him to be much concerned about how this job was to be handled; it wasn't any of his business really. It didn't make much difference whether it worked out properly or not.

He let himself slump in his saddle as the patrol moved forward, paying no attention to details although he was well aware that Addison was issuing sharp orders. They rode without flankers, the Lieutenant in the lead with Featherstone beside him. Barry simply found himself a convenient place in the line. For the moment he liked it that way; he even slept a little as his horse walked slowly through the darkness.

Then he knew that the column was having a little trouble groping its way through the broken country. Twice Sawdust led them into winding gulleys that had been avoided on the earlier scout but each time a correction was made as soon as the general direction showed the error. On the second bad move Barry found his drowsiness leaving him. A cold wind had started to drift in out of the northwest and it wasn't comfortable to sleep, particularly in the saddle. Anyway he was wondering about those mistakes Sawdust had made. He had a shrewd hunch that they had been done purposely. Sawdust was trying to make Addison feel that they needed Barry.

"Dam' fool!" Barry murmured to himself, trying to feel disgusted but pleased instead. "He oughta know I don't care about it. So what?"

He tried to force his mind to other considerations. Would it turn out that his father had actually made a deal with Jess Conway? How would Linda feel about things by this time? Maybe she was long since married. Probably had a family by now. Three years of war made a lot of difference to people. To himself, for example. Who would have expected that Tom Barry would find himself riding through a cold winter night in Colorado—or wherever this miserable spot actually was—behind a pig-headed Kansas abolitionist and a crazy wildman?

Addison showed good judgment then. In spite of Featherstone's insistence that they were close to the line of bluffs he halted the column for a ten minute rest. "Rest your horses, men," he called back cautiously. "We'll move up slowly after that. Walk most of the time. We may need all we can get out of the animals later."

Moments later he walked back to where Barry had dropped to the ground to stretch out. "You all right, Sergeant?" he asked. "No! Don't get up!"

"I'm fine, sir. Why?"

"You've had mighty little rest since we left Fort Laramie. I hoped you'd get a bit while I rode with Featherstone."

Barry grimaced to himself in the darkness. Was this the pig-headed Kansas abolitionist talking? "I reckon I had a small nap in the saddle," he admitted.

"I hoped you would. Do you feel up to taking over the lead when we move again? Featherstone thinks we'll be coming within sight of the creek bottom before long."

"I'll be ready, sir," Barry told him.

It was a little after midnight when they began the climb into the crag country, making another brief halt for rest and to pass new orders. Herbert Rossiter was given the job of handling the spare horses, his objections little more than a normal show of ill-humor. Addison wanted every fighting man free to use his weapons.

Barry judged that the ascent continued along almost exactly the same line he had used earlier with Sawdust. He wasn't sure how the scout had found the same unmarked path in the darkness but it appeared that he had done it. They even halted the troops at the spot where earlier they had left their horses.

"We'll see them just ahead, Lieutenant," he told Addison as the halt was called. "Maybe we can guess what's happened since our last look."

The three of them moved forward quietly. It was not likely that the Indians would have posted any lookouts among the crags, there being no likely prospect of white troops using the area, but it was well to play it as safe as possible. The longer the hostiles were ignorant of new enemies in the area the better the chances for those outnumbered new enemies—and for the badly battered old ones.

The waning moon had not yet risen so only the cold light of the November stars helped to dispel the blackness. Stark shadows made it hard to tell which was a butte and which was a patch of flat ground. The crags had looked fearsome in daylight; at night they were merely confusing. Then Barry suddenly knew that they had crossed the summit and were staring out across the flat valley to the south.

For a moment or two he couldn't quite figure it out. In the darkness distances were deceiving and perspective disappeared. Then he got it. The black of the little basin was punctured by six small fires. One was directly in front of the three watchers on the bluffs. Another was directly beyond it but at least a mile farther away. On either side two other tiny flames showed. The rest was inky blackness.

"What in the world?" Addison whispered. "Are those . . . ?"

"Looks like the Cheyennes have got theirselves a ring of picket fires around the wagons," Sawdust broke in. "It didn't figger that they'd make any big fight before daybreak but they ain't lettin' the white folks fergit what a hell of a bad place they're in."

Almost as he spoke they could hear a gunshot bang somewhere in the distance. Then another shot sounded off to the right a little, both sounds swept away quickly by the freshening breeze.

"Indians will keep scouts out all night, sir," Barry explained. "They'll keep the wagoners awake and nervous.

When the attack comes at dawn there's more chance of the defenders getting panicky."

"Then none of these fires are at the wagon camp?"

"Nope." Sawdust was positive about it. "The wagons are corralled jest about on a line between them two fires straight ahead of us. Right smack in the middle of the circle."

"Obviously that earlier idea about slipping in to join the wagoners won't work," Addison muttered grimly. "They're surrounded. I think we'd better take the offensive. Perhaps we can surprise the enemy."

"Ain't much chance o' that," Sawdust told him. "Troops on shod hosses jest don't sneak up on Injuns. Not often, anyhow."

"Then we'll adopt the opposite strategy!" Addison exclaimed, suddenly showing excitement. "They don't suspect our presence. They're completely sure of themselves and of their own plans. We'll hit them hard with plenty of noise. It should be just the thing!"

"Jest the thing fer the Cheyennes!" Sawdust growled. "They'd like it fine!"

"Why?" The old snap was back in the question. Evidently Sawdust's obvious contempt had gotten the Lieutenant's back up. He was remembering that he didn't think much of these men who had been placed under his orders.

Sawdust answered steadily. "Mister, there ain't no better runnin' fighter than a Cheyenne. If we bust in on 'em, usin' their slashin' style o' fightin' we'll be givin' 'em all the odds. I don't figger it would be a good stunt even if'n we had more guns than they've got. With the odds about four to one against us it's crazier'n hell!"

70

"Mind your manners, Private Featherstone! And you'd better recall that these are savages we're going to attack. Ignorant savages who think only in terms of plundering unarmed and helpless civilians. They've never been known to stand before a cavalry charge."

Barry knew a feeling of sick helplessness at the Lieutenant's tone. Still he managed to keep his own voice quiet as he intervened. "This is not a cavalry unit, Lieutenant. Our men have no training in such tactics, and we don't really know where the Indian camp is."

"I thought you reported that it was . . ."

"The main force was at about the present location of that nearer fire on your right, sir. That was before dark. There are five other fires. We have no way of knowing how they've distributed their forces and we don't have time to find out."

"Then we'll attack the two closer spots. We should be able to inflict considerable punishment on the enemy before they know what is happening to them. At the same time we let the wagon people know that we're out here. It will relieve us of the risk of being fired on by friends when we approach the wagons later."

Barry decided not to argue the point. Addison was getting the bit in his teeth. The only thing to do was to go along with him and try to keep his plans from becoming as suicidal as they sounded. "We'd better bring up the men, sir," he suggested. "We should hit the enemy before they begin to gather themselves for their own attack."

"Get them," Addison ordered. "Private Featherstone and I will remain here for further observation."

Chapter 7

Barry took only a few seconds to tell the men what was being planned. Then the little force moved up among the crags, halting when Addison's voice came out of the gloom.

"We'll move right in for the attack," he announced crisply. "The detachment attacking the fire to the right will need a little more time to get into position. The other group will move accordingly, waiting to hear the first sounds of attack before making their own assault. Sergeant, have you explained the plan to everyone?"

"Yes, sir. But wouldn't it be wiser to make one attack, Lieutenant? Our force is pretty small to risk dividing it."

"I assume full responsibility for the decision, Sergeant. Two bold attacks out of the darkness! The hostiles will believe that they have been hit by a large force. Surprise will carry us through before they recover from their panic. A saber charge in the dead of night is something an Indian doesn't understand."

Featherstone's grunt sounded almost comic. "Saber charge!" he exploded. "Hell, mister, we ain't got no sabers!"

For a few seconds Addison made no reply. Barry knew that he was annoyed at the undisciplined outburst but was also embarrassed at not having noticed this detail.

"I might have known!" he snapped after a pause. "I suppose, Sergeant Barry, that you have a perfectly ridiculous explanation for ignoring regulations?"

"I don't believe it's ridiculous," Barry told him steadily.

"For one thing we're not cavalry. A mixed lot of infantry and militia riding guard duty works out its own ideas. My squad prefers to use the revolver."

"Revolver! They're not issued to the ranks, particularly not in this part of the country."

"Yes, sir. My men carry their own personal weapons."

"Purchased with what? Confederate money?"

It took a little effort for Barry to ignore the sarcasm, particularly when he could hear Rossiter's grunt of approval. "I took mine from a dead Sioux," he replied. "The other men acquired theirs in their own way, sir."

"All honest methods, I don't doubt." Addison was being his sarcastic best.

"I did not inquire, sir."

"I'm sure you didn't. You may rest assured that my report will request an inquiry, Sergeant." He paused as though to let this threat sink in, then went on in a milder tone, "We will attack as already ordered. I will lead the attack on the right hand fire. Corporal Wirtz will ride as my second in command, bringing with him all troopers properly armed with sabers.

"Sergeant Barry, your men are to proceed more slowly. When you hear us attack you will attack promptly. Perhaps you can make enough noise to atone for your striking power. May I remind you that this is a direct order. The attack must be pressed. Failure to do so carries the usual penalty.

"Mister Rossiter, I'm requesting that you continue to take charge of the spare horses. Follow Sergeant Barry's detachment until the attack begins. Then try to reach the wagons. Identify yourself as you go in so they won't fire at you. Tell them what we're doing and have them ready to support us after we break through the enemy lines."

Barry suppressed a wry smile. Addison managed to let everyone know that he'd learned his tactics out of a book, even though his general plan was not too bad. It might even work. At least the man had nerve enough to take on the big bite. He was getting ready to lead five men against what might well be the main Indian camp.

A distant shot sounded then and Addison quickly explained to the men who had not heard the earlier sounds. "The hostiles are merely keeping the wagoners nerved up. Pay no attention to such demonstrations as we move in. Are you ready, Corporal?"

"Yes, sir," Wirtz growled. "How far do you reckon it is to that fire, sir?"

"Don't worry about details. I've spent a lot of time with Private Featherstone reviewing the situation. Forward!"

Shadowy figures began to separate themselves from the huddle of troopers. When five of them were in single file, ready to hit the downgrade, Addison rode ahead to lead them. Barry heaved a sigh of relief. At least the Lieutenant was sure enough of himself that he wasn't going to take Sawdust with him.

"Well, Sergeant?" Rossiter demanded. "Do we wait here all night?"

"We let Lieutenant Addison get a small start," Barry told him. "And that's the last I want to hear out of you until we reach the wagons. You've got a job to do this time. Just do it and keep your trap shut!"

"Want me to shet it fer him, Sarge?" Samuels asked hopefully.

"If necessary."

Sawdust broke in at that point. "We'd better git movin', Sarge. That fool Lieutenant has got it all figgered out that the Injuns has got theirselves all divided up neat around them six fires. He thinks there'll be six or eight of 'em to deal with."

"And you don't agree?"

"Nope. I got a hunch he's goin' to hit the main band. Seems like we oughta git our chore cleaned up in case he needs help."

Rossiter started to say something but choked it off as a trooper swung his horse toward him. Barry simply said, "Let's go, boys. We'll ride until we're about half way to the fire. There's enough wind to cover the noise, I hope."

It seemed to him that the wind was getting colder by the minute as he followed Sawdust down the rough slope. He hoped it would get stronger. Without it Addison had little chance of getting close to the enemy. And he would need full surprise.

When he halted the squad they were among the rolling swells which marked the broad valley, the fires only visible at times as they found themselves on the same level. "Walk the horses," he ordered. "Be ready to mount. And put caps on the cylinders under your hammers. We might need every shot we can muster."

It helped a little to walk instead of ride. Fighting an overpowering weariness was better than having the wind bring the shakes to tired muscles. Finally Sawdust hissed, "Seems like we oughta take a look, Sarge. Mebbe I could do it alone. You better stick here to give me a hand if'n I git into a tight."

"Everybody will be ready," Barry assured him. "But don't waste time. The Lieutenant ought to be getting close to that other fire by this time."

As soon as Sawdust moved ahead on foot Samuels, who had taken over the scout's horse, suggested, "What about shovin' on real slow and careful, Sarge. Seems like we might need to give him a hand mighty fast."

"That's exactly what we're going to do. Handle your horses carefully. No noise—but be ready to get into the saddle in a hurry. Pass the word to Rossiter. He's to break for the wagons at the first sign of trouble."

They crept forward another three minutes. By that time Barry knew that the fire they were approaching had been built at the summit of one of those low swells they had been crossing. He could see no sign of life near its glow but he could tell that it was burning very low. Probably Sawdust's guess had been correct. Most of these fires were simply intended to make the wagon folks feel surrounded and threatened during the night. There was no important part of the hostile force at the site.

Ladou's whisper came to him in the darkness. "The Lieutenant—I t'eenk he is in trouble."

"Quiet!" Barry ordered. Ladou was right. Addison's men were about to attack the bulk of the war party. Now their only chance was complete surprise, a break-through, and retreat to the wagons. They would need plenty of luck.

Then Sawdust came running back, making no attempt at concealment and calling out in a voice loud enough to be recognized by men with nervous trigger fingers. "It's a fake up there. They left just one man to tend fire."

Nobody needed to ask him what had happened to the

lone Indian and there was no opportunity for questions. A clatter of sound broke out just behind Barry and he had to grab his horse to keep the animal from bolting. The men with him were having similar problems but Strauss let go with a volley of German curses, switching suddenly to English as he added, "It's Rossiter. He's breaking for the wagon camp!"

The fat man was shouting wildly at the horses he was taking with him, urging them forward. Nobody could believe that the animals had bolted with him. They were simply too tired for such a thing. He had heard that the way to personal safety was now clear so he was taking it. At the same time he was setting up an alarm that would ruin whatever chance Addison and his men would have had to surprise the Indian camp.

"Mount up!" Barry shouted. "The other squad's in trouble. Let's give 'em a hand."

A shot sounded from the dark area where he knew the wagon corral to be and they could hear Rossiter squealing identification and telling the defenders not to shoot. Then firing broke out to the west of them and they swung their horses to take a direction that would put them part way between the two lots of noise. Barry did not need to give any orders. They knew as well as he did that they could not reach the other squad in time to help much with the fight at the Indian camp. All they could hope to do was to join them in retreat and try to beat off pursuit.

"Don't try even one shot with the carbines," Barry called as they raced into position. "Close work and fast with the six-shooters. Don't aim at the wrong targets!"

He could hear scattered shots in the distance behind his

men but guessed that this would be the harassing fire of the warriors who had been posted at the fires. They were probably firing blindly into the wagon circle, not knowing what the noise was about but intent upon adding to the confusion.

It seemed to him that the night had shaded out just a little. There was still no real show of dawn but the blackness was not quite so intense. He could make out the forms of the men around him so he assumed that there would be light enough for the kind of hasty shooting that would be done.

He shouted an order to halt and the squad pulled up in good formation, all of them listening to the sound of fighting that was sweeping toward them. There actually wasn't much shooting, only an occasional blast from some sort of heavy weapon like a musket or perhaps a shotgun. Probably Addison's men had used their carbines after discovering that they were in trouble with the proposed saber attack. There had been no time to reload so they were retreating before an Indian attack which hadn't really had time to muster full strength. It didn't seem likely that too many of the savages had been able to mount up promptly enough to undertake a full pursuit.

"Move up," Barry ordered after a moment of listening. "Keep spaced out. When we see our boys let them know we're here and let them through our line to reload. Then give the Cheyennes hell with the revolvers. That'll hold 'em for a bit and we'll fall back." He hoped that the strategy would work out as well as he was trying to make it sound.

It didn't take long to find out. Scarcely had the new advance begun when they could make out the forms of riders coming toward them at a full gallop. Barry yelled instructions to them and knew that only two troopers had slipped through his line in response to the hail. Several pursuing Indians went down before the blast of revolver fire that met them but then Barry saw a flurry of action on his right. Some kind of hand-to-hand fight was going on there.

He spurred his horse toward the scene, knowing that one of the troopers was right beside him, yelling for others to hold fire in that area. For a moment it was hard to tell which was friend and which was enemy but one of the struggling figures separated itself from the tangle and let out a yell that was all Indian. Barry promptly blasted him down with a close range shot from the Colt. The other trooper was firing also, somehow seeming to know which was a target and which was a friend.

Suddenly the violent little battle subsided and Barry swung from the saddle to reach for the man who lay there on the ground. His fingers slipped in blood but he picked the man up, knowing that for all the bulk of the overcoat this was a man of slender build. By that time he had help. Gerhardt Strauss was the man who had sided him in the fight and now the Austrian helped boost the rescued man into Barry's saddle.

"I think you've picked up our good Lieutenant," he whispered huskily. "Maybe you want to leave him here? No?"

"Hold him in the saddle while I climb up," Barry said tiredly. "He's out cold."

Strauss did not argue. He had come up with a good suggestion but it didn't seem to make any difference to him if the Sergeant didn't care to take it. He followed orders and went back to his own horse, a sudden silence on the prairie indicating that the Cheyennes had retreated in some haste after running into the fire of Barry's troopers.

The dawn was now showing more definitely in the east, giving men a chance to see something more than mere shadows. Barry shouted a quick order at Sawdust and Samuels who were starting forward as though to follow the retreating Indians. "Don't get drawn into anything! There may be another band between us and the wagons. Just make sure that we're not leaving any wounded behind us but then head for cover." He was already turning to ride toward the distant wagons, Strauss and Ladou closing in as escorts.

"How many of that other lot got through?" he asked, speaking to no one in particular. "I thought I saw two— besides this one."

"Two it was," Strauss agreed. "No more."

"Any of our boys hurt?"

"No. Neither of us, I know. You saw the others."

That was the way of it. His squad had continued to be mighty lucky. The other group hadn't fared so well. Three of them were missing and Lieutenant Addison was wounded, perhaps seriously. Maybe he was actually dead. Barry decided that he wouldn't try to find out until they had reached the wagons.

Sawdust and Samuels closed in on them quickly, reporting with some grimness that they had found no sign of the missing men. Evidently the casualties had occurred in the first burst of fighting. The men who had come through the first fire had managed to reach the point where Barry's squad had rescued them.

"Poor galoots never had a chance," Sawdust growled.

"When that fat sonofabitch busted loose from us he stirred up the Injuns and they was awake and waitin'. I think we oughta hang the bastard."

"A mere opinion from the ranks," a faint voice said from somewhere in the folds of Barry's overcoat. "Official view is he's an important man. Got to give him all help . . ." The voice died away and Barry could feel a new limpness in the man he was carrying.

"He ain't dead anyhow," Sawdust commented after a moment of surprised silence. "I'm kinda glad—not that I ever thought I'd be."

A couple of bearded men carrying rifles came out between the wagons to meet them. They were followed by Corporal Wirtz who was motioning for the oncoming group to swing toward a different opening in the wagon circle. "Take yer wounded man to that first wagon with the burnt top," he yelled. "Where's everybody else?"

"Get lookouts posted and be ready," Barry shouted to the wagoners. "We've got to expect an attack and not long from now." Then he swung in beside Wirtz who was exclaiming at the realization that Lieutenant Addison was the man being brought in.

"I thought he was a goner," he said in a low tone. "I seen him go down but I had three of the hellions hacking away at me just then. Wasn't much I could do." Then he snapped, "How come you bastards busted out too soon? It let us run right smack into a hornets' nest!"

"We didn't. Our friend Rossiter bolted when he found out that we didn't have anybody in front of us. Our fire was a dummy. Only one Indian there and Sawdust disposed of him without a sound."

"You mean it was that fat polecat got our boys killed?"

"No doubt about it. But don't start anything right now. We've still got Indians to fight. By the way, who's the other man who got clear?"

"Welland, and he didn't get off clean. Hole in his leg. I dunno how bad."

They moved inside the wagon circle then and several men lifted the Lieutenant down from Barry's grip, carrying him across to where two women were bandaging Trooper Welland's leg. Barry slid from the saddle and wiped blood from his hands before digging into saddlebags for extra ammunition. Then he waved aside the excited questions of the teamsters who surrounded him, firing brisk orders at Wirtz.

"Corporal, take charge of defense on this side of the corral. Find out which of the civilians have repeating weapons. Then space them out along with our men who have revolvers. Don't let too many men with single shot guns be together. We can't leave a soft place for an attack to break through."

Wirtz stared for a moment but then grinned. He was turning to obey orders when Barry asked, "Where's Sawdust?"

"Outside. Watchin' the hostiles."

"Fine. We'll have due warning then." He swung to snap his words at the dirty bewhiskered men who were staring at him on all sides. "Get into good defense posts, all of you. Those Cheyennes are plenty sore and they were primed for this attack anyhow. You heard what I told the corporal about repeaters. Follow orders and we'll get through this somehow."

Herbert Rossiter took that moment to show himself. He pushed through the crowd as pompously as his rumpled appearance permitted. "That's enough from you, Barry! You can't come into my train and give orders in such a highhanded fashion!"

Barry crooked a finger at Private Strauss. "Keep that man quiet!" he ordered. "If he tries to interfere in any way with our defense of this wagon circle—shoot him!"

"A pleasure, Sarge," Strauss said, bringing up his six-gun.

Barry added one fast remark. "Three men died because you broke loose a little while ago. That leaves seven of us who figure you killed them."

Rossiter gulped hard. Then he took a look at Strauss and headed for the other side of the circle. Barry jerked a thumb toward the wagon behind him. "Into your places! Move!"

Sawdust met him in the opening between wagons. "It won't be long," the scout reported. "They're gittin' their-selves frenzied up."

"Any sign of the missing men?"

"Not alive. I took a good look. Seems like I'd see prisoners but there wasn't none."

"Better that way. Take over here; I'm going to see how Addison's doing."

He moved through between packs of merchandise that had been turned into defense works, pausing where two women now worked over Lieutenant Addison. The officer's uniform had been cut away to expose wounds on one thigh and the other upper arm. The leg wound appeared to be from a musket ball but the arm wound was a nasty slash that might have been done with a lance. He had lost a lot of blood and the two volunteer nurses were having trouble with that problem as they tried to put on compresses that would stop some of the flow.

"Broken bones?" Barry asked quietly as he peered across the tops of their heads.

"We think not," a calm voice with a slight accent told him. He wondered vaguely about the accent but then his thoughts changed abruptly to something quite different. The other nurse had looked up at his question and he found himself staring into the brown, startled eyes of Linda Conway.

Out of his own astonishment several ideas fought for precedence. He knew that the girl's presence had to mean something that required explanation. He also knew that he didn't have time to think about it. Because he realized that she believed him dead he dropped other matters to say—so calmly that he wondered whether it was his own voice he heard in his ears, "I'm alive, Linda. Try to see that this man stays that way too."

There was no opportunity to say more. The distant whoop of the Cheyennes was partly covered by the murmur which swept around the defense line. A lot of explanations would have to wait. Unless the defenders were might lucky there would be a good many explanations that could be forgotten. Dead men don't explain nor listen to explanations.

CHAPTER 8

Sawdust was waiting when Barry climbed up on a wagon to look out. "Seems like the varmints had a mite o' trouble makin' up their minds, Sarge," he said with a wry grin. "They sure done a hell of a lot o' pow-wowin' before they got mounted up."

Barry stared at the line of barbaric figures that was beginning to stretch out across the prairie as the Cheyennes started to form their attack circle. "Any idea what's bothering them?"

"Only a guess. There's two lots of 'em, ye know. Last night it seemed like they mighta been gittin' jealous about who was runnin' this show. Now I got a hunch we messed up their politics fer 'em by killin' one of the big chiefs in the mornin' fightin'. They're plenty mad but they ain't actin' the way mad Injuns oughta."

"Fine. They're hurt already. Maybe discouraged. And they don't know how much of a force moved in to help the wagoners. We'll try to give them a quick hint that this is no place for discouraged Indians." He glanced around at the wagon circle and added, "Pass the word for a few of the men with good rifles to start pecking away at the big feather bonnets as soon as they get within extreme range. Nobody else is to fire. Rifles only when they make their false charge. Carbines and revolvers stay quiet until the real thing."

Sawdust grinned. "Most o' these wagon fellers are carryin' the Springfield. Rifle, not musket. If'n they can aim them Minie balls like they oughta we could see some real unhappy Injuns." He moved away on his errand, leaving Barry to try for some kind of clarity in his own thoughts. It wasn't easy.

The Indians played their deadly game according to formula, riding in a wide circle while they screamed themselves into the proper frenzy for attack. Barry watched narrowly, recalling what he had seen in earlier attacks and what Sawdust had told him. It occurred to him that the only advantage the white man held in the Indian wars was really a matter of superior brutality. Indians handled their fighting with a certain amount of artistic flair, risking their lives foolishly because it was according to code to do so, or refusing to take risks of good military value because no coup could be counted. They were savage fighters but not very practical nor efficient. The white man killed far more scientifically and with no regard for anything except the brutal extermination of his enemy. This morning Barry was planning to be just as coldly efficient as possible in taking full advantage of Indian weaknesses.

When the riding circle began to narrow he yelled his warning. "Open up with just a couple of the best rifles! You know who you are. Worry 'em!"

When the circle began to show signs of switching to headlong attack he shouted again, "Don't be fooled. Only rifles hit 'em when they rush. The rest of you wait till you've got 'em close!"

The Cheyennes were letter perfect. They made their false rush at just about the point Barry had expected, the maneuver calculated to draw rifle fire against the leaders who thus proved their valor. Then the main attack would come in against empty weapons. The Indians had been perfecting this strategy for years and the taste of repeating weapons had not yet done anything to make them change their tactics.

For an instant Barry thought the pattern would break. The teamsters hit hard with their rifles, knocking four of the posturing savages from their ponies. It almost spoiled the strategy of defense because that accurate rifle fire made the already skittish Cheyennes falter.

Then a burly chief wearing full eagle plumes rallied them with angry shouts. They came on again, the bulk of them at the upstream side of the corral. Barry shouted orders for a couple of his men to move into the threatened part of the line, the shift being made just as the Indians came into revolver range. At that point Barry could only hope that the rest of the defense would keep the feinting attacks from becoming real ones; he had all he could do right in front of him.

It did not last long. The original blast of carbine and rifle fire had been followed by a rattle of revolver shots as mounted Indians jumped over fallen comrades to plunge into the wagon circle. Barry killed one almost directly behind his defense position. Several others fell partly inside the circle. Then the yells took on a new note. The Indians were in retreat, trying to take their dead and wounded with them.

"No mercy!" Barry shouted. "Kill every one you can. Kill him now and he can't attack tomorrow." Admiration for savage bravery in carrying away casualties was all right but it was not very practical for an enemy to be too much taken with it.

He grimaced to himself as the thought crossed his mind. This was more of the white man's brutality. Efficient killing was all that counted. Indians observed certain courtesies in such a matter but a white man didn't. At least this white man didn't propose to do so now.

It was difficult to see what was happening now. The

smoke had become a gray pall that shut out even the opposite side of the circle. Barry moved in beside a powder-blackened Sawdust. "Think they're on the run?" he asked.

"Them what's left is. Might as well holler fer the boys to stop blastin' away."

The firing gradually died as the word was passed around. Barry made a quick survey of the part of the circle which had taken the brunt of the assault. Two men were bandaging wounded friends, in each case the wounded man sounding reasonably cheerful about it. At another point a bearded man lay on his back with an arrow sticking out of his chest. It was clear enough that he was dead.

The smoke began to lift a little and Barry went out through it with Sawdust and Ladou. He needed to know what the hostiles might be planning to do next.

It didn't take much study to know that they were not going to do much of anything. Already the few who had threatened the other angles of the wagon circle were returning to join the badly battered main body where the defeated warriors had retreated with their dead and wounded.

"Beat the livin' hell out of 'em that time!" Sawdust muttered as they watched the distant scene. "I can't count more'n fourteen of 'em left alive. And some of 'em is wounded. Last night we figgered there was forty in the two parties. That's goin' to make 'em think twice before they git gay with the next lot o' wagons!"

Barry was searching the surrounding ridges for more Indians. It did not seem possible that the enemy had suffered quite so heavily. He knew that the early morning fight had probably accounted for a half dozen warriors; perhaps more if Addison's original attack had been effective. It still meant that the Cheyennes had lost fifty percent of their strength in the attack on the wagons. Then he started counting the Indian dead and decided that it had really happened.

"Keep an eye on 'em," he told Sawdust. "I'll try to get these wagons moving. No telling when more Indians might come along." He was thinking about that first bit of Indian sign they had seen.

Back inside the wagon circle he came face to face with a heavy bodied man whose iron gray stubble was streaked with black at one corner of his mouth. Barry grinned at the puzzled light in the big man's dark eyes. "You heard it right, Jess," he greeted, extending a grimy hand. "I'm alive and here. Looks like you must have been biting open cartridges with the best of them."

Jess Conway put his free hand to his mouth as though expecting to feel the powder stains. "I've still got teeth," he said with a short laugh. "I can show 'em when I have to." His laugh broke off as he added in a lower tone, "Seems like you showed some fangs already this morning, Tom. And I don't mean in the Indian fight."

"You're talking about my little fuss with Rossiter? I'm going to show more than fangs to that polecat! How come you're traveling with his wagons? I thought you'd be . . ."

"He's my partner. When I heard that you'd been killed out here I threw in with him. He took over all of Bill's holdings, being as there was nobody else to . . ."

The two of them exchanged glances before Conway exclaimed, "This changes a lot of things! We'd better get together real fast and figure a few things out. I'm beginning to think there's been a . . ."

Barry was also beginning to think a few things but he had no chance to express them. A lanky, loose-jointed man who wore his brown hair long beneath the brim of a tall hat broke in with a sullen, "All right to hitch up? It looks like the Injuns are pullin' out, and there's snow in the air."

He was right on both counts. Barry had forgotten about the threat in the weather but now he knew that that danger had to be taken into account. It would be bad enough for wagons to be caught on the trail in snow. Back here where there were no trails it would be a lot worse.

"This is Abe Shingle, Barry," Conway said, still staring thoughtfully. "He knows his wagons. Worked for Rossiter back in the Ohio Valley."

Barry nodded, noting this extra bit of information even as he appraised the rawboned wagoner. Somehow the man made him think of Sawdust. They were built a lot alike. In their own ways they were probably equally dangerous. "Move out as soon as you can," he agreed. "If the Indians come back we can always pull up and fight again."

The wagon boss turned away and Barry called after him, "Can you make room in the wagons for the wounded? You might shift a couple of loads so you could put them all together." He thought he should make it as a sort of suggestion rather than an order. Better to get along with Shingle. If the man didn't turn out to be willing there would be time to get tough.

"I'll talk to you later, Jess," he told Conway. "I'd better see to a few things."

He had to see to quite a lot of things. Before the wagons moved he needed to know how many men were with the outfit and how they might be used in case of a fresh attack. He had to arrange for his own men to set up their marching order. The wounded had to be readied for travel. Back on the prairie three dead troopers were entitled to decent burial. Those were the big duties. He didn't even try to think about the dozens of smaller details.

He found Ladou and Wirtz helping to set up a dressing station for the wounded. Welland had fought the Indians from a position under a wagon, his earlier wound ignored. Now he was being treated by a blonde woman of perhaps thirty, the same woman who had helped Linda with Lieutenant Addison.

"Just a little hole in the leg," she was telling the Texan with that odd little accent making her cheerfulness sound all the more real. "You are a lucky man that you did not bleed to death before someone found that you needed attention."

"And careless," Barry broke in over her shoulder. "With such a pretty nurse on hand he should have yowled for attention a lot earlier."

The blonde woman turned to smile up at him, showing good white teeth and remarkable pale blue eyes. "Hello," she greeted. "You are the rebel, no? I mean the Galvanized Yankee. It is good that you arrived when you did. We needed you."

She bent over her work again, not looking up as she added, "I am Kate Hennessey."

The name didn't seem to fit either her appearance or her talk but Barry didn't ask questions. He glanced down at Welland and saw that the man was in some pain but in little danger. "Able to talk a bit, Welland?" he asked.

"Of course he is!" Kate Hennessey snapped. "You heard him complaining, I am sure!"

The trooper managed a weak grin. Obviously he had lost a lot of blood before stopping to get his wound treated. "Can't talk much, Sarge," he muttered. "She don't give me a chance. Real gabby."

"Ingrate," the lady said with a quick laugh.

"Tell me what you remember about the beginning of your attack," Barry said. "I've got to look for bodies."

"Which ones didn't make it?"

"Brady, O'Connell and Peace. Addison's hurt plenty bad."

"That's rough. We was in a hell of a mess when that noise busted loose. They tell me Rossiter done it."

"Right. But don't worry about it now. Where did you hit the Indians?"

"They hit us when we was still mebbe a hundred yards short of their fire. We drove through the best we could. I dunno when any of the other boys got hit. It was dark and I was plenty damned busy."

Barry nodded. "Take care of him, Katie," he said quietly. Then he went on to where Wirtz was helping with a couple of the lightly wounded wagoners. He caught a sidelong glance from Linda Conway who seemed to be taking charge of this lot of wounded but he made no attempt to talk with her. Instead he asked Wirtz the same question he had asked Welland, getting the same answer.

By that time he knew that Samuels had taken an arrow through the fleshy part of his calf but that the wound was not serious. One teamster was dead but none of the other injuries seemed critical. Only Addison, Welland and three men who had been wounded in earlier fighting would have to be transported as invalids. Shingle was already giving orders for loading them into wagons, the more lightly wounded ready to lend a hand with the driving. The defense of the wagon circle had been pretty fortunate in its general results.

Featherstone rode in then to announce that the Cheyennes were moving away to the east, taking their dead and wounded with them. Only a few scouts lingered behind the main force as though unwilling to abandon the attack.

Barry promptly called Ladou and Wirtz. "You'd better go along on burial detail, Corporal," he said shortly. "They're your men. You'd better know what happened. We'll borrow a couple of shovels."

Featherstone led the way straight toward the spot where Addison had led his men into trouble. Halfway across the valley they saw the hostile scouts start toward them as though toying with the idea of a last assault.

"We'll watch them but we'll keep going," Barry said. "It'll be a good way to find out how much guts they've got left." There were six of the warriors so it did not seem like too much of a gamble to risk attack.

Moments later several of the wagoners rode out from the wagon circle and took positions where they could take a hand in any fight that might develop. Immediately the Indians halted, not retreating but not advancing any further.

"Stalemate," Barry grunted. "Let's get on with it."

They knew what he meant. Certainly none of them had been looking forward to this job with anything but revulsion. The troopers must have fallen right in the middle of the main Indian camp—and long before the Cheyenne attack on the wagons. The savages would have had plenty of time to do their worst.

It did not take long to find the bodies. Barry glanced just once before ordering, "Dig here in this sand bank. One grave. Shallow."

The threat of the distant Cheyennes made the grisly chore a little more bearable. Exhausted men working with death just across the valley have little time for emotion. They simply scooped out a shallow grave and dumped the hacked bodies into it.

Barry found time for a fleeting thought that O'Connell, the loud hater of secession, would probably have objected to burial beside the rebel Brady. Not that Brady was much of a secessionist. He was simply a Texas boy who had done what his fellows were doing in a time of vast excitement. Brady had had no more political feeling than had Peace, the Ohioan. In a sense they had been the victims of hatreds stirred up by the O'Connells and the Addisons—their counterparts on the opposite side. Not that it made any difference now. It was hard to tell which man was which. The Cheyennes had left only revolting remnants of human flesh.

Sawdust broke in then. "Injuns pullin' out, Sarge. Mebbe they don't like this snow."

Barry hadn't even noticed that the big flakes were beginning to fall all around him. "It'll hide the grave," he said shortly. "Let's get back to the wagons."

The teamsters had wheeled into line when they reached the camp. Jess Conway hailed Barry from the seat of the first wagon. "What's the plan, Tom?" he asked. "Are you going to stay with us? Shingle don't know the country so we'll be might glad if you see us through."

"Our orders are to get you into Colorado militia country," Barry told him. "With Lieutenant Addison wounded we may have to stretch the orders a bit and stay longer."

"Good. By the way, I'm driving because we're short of men. Two killed in the first attack. You've seen our wounded. Two of them can't help much and everybody's worn out. If we hadn't happened to pick up a couple of ranchers who got burned out in raids we'd be having to use women as drivers."

"And we'd handle the job too!" a voice said briskly from behind him. The woman who peered out from behind the canvas flap was no longer young but she wore her years well, the gray of her hair only providing a striking frame for dark eyes that showed plenty of life for all their weariness. A smudge across her cheek and on one side of her nose made her seem even more like a school-girl instead of the mother of a grown daughter.

"Hi, Mrs. Conway," Barry greeted with real feeling. "I wondered what happened to you when I saw Jess and Linda. But I didn't get time to ask. Things were a mite busy about then. Are you still keeping everybody licked into proper shape?"

She smiled her appreciation of his tone. "I gave up on almost everybody a long time ago. Nobody seems to make sense."

"Don't believe her," Conway chuckled. "She's as worried about the country's affairs as anybody but that don't stop her telling me what to do."

Barry grinned. "I hope you obey orders. Mostly she's

right." He swung his horse suddenly, keeping back the urge to tell her that it had been a disappointment to him not to have continued looking forward to being her son-in-law. Somehow it didn't seem like the kind of thing that needed saying just now.

"Might as well roll," he told Conway. "We'll travel with our scouts out. I'll talk to you again after I speak to the Lieutenant."

He signaled for Sawdust to ride out ahead and then drifted back along the line of wagons, taking curt nods from Rossiter and Shingle as well as more friendly greetings from various drivers. He found Addison in a wagon near the end of the line. The wounded man had been made comfortable on a pile of blankets atop a load of flour sacks. Linda Conway had climbed up to crouch beside him under a rag of canvas top which had been only partly burned away. She was letting him take small sips of water from a canteen which was probably his own. When Barry pulled up at the rear of the wagon she did not even look around. It seemed pretty obvious that she had not changed her mind about Tom Barry. To her he was still a man who had made his choice of sides in the big war, a choice which had gone against her and against his country. She had put it that way four years earlier and Barry could almost hear the thought repeating itself in her mind. It still disturbed him.

CHAPTER 9

"We're moving out, Lieutenant," Barry reported quietly. "The Cheyennes have apparently retreated."

"What of our casualties?" Addison asked in a weak

voice. "Did you . . . ?"

"Buried, sir. Brady, Peace and O'Connell. Samuels and Welland are slightly wounded but can do service in an emergency."

There was a pause before Addison repeated the names of the dead, his voice little more than a whisper. Then he asked, "Did all of them die in that first attack?"

"Yes, sir. Samuels got an arrow wound when the savages attacked the wagons. We beat them off handsomely, sir."

"So I've been told. Well done, Sergeant. Were our dead mutilated?"

"No, sir." Barry decided that a small lie would do no harm. If Addison could rest any better thinking that way it wouldn't make any difference to the dead men. "What about your own injuries, sir?"

"Flesh wounds only. No broken bones. Much less serious than I deserve, I'm afraid. The assault was a mistake— even forgetting the alarm that ruined our surprise. I was rash."

Barry didn't think it was a good idea to dwell on that subject. "We're heading southwest, sir. Featherstone thinks we might strike a branch of the South Platte that has water in it. The train is in bad shape for water. If the snow continues we'll make out somehow but the stock need it bad."

"How far until we'll meet the militia?"

"Hard to tell, sir."

"Do your best, Sergeant. It's up to you now."

Barry wondered just how hard it had been for the Lieutenant to say that—or to make such a complete admission of his own errors. Before he could give the thought much time, however, Linda Conway broke in, twisting around on her awkward perch to face him for the first time. "I'm sure the Lieutenant realizes what he is forced to do!" she snapped. "Only the most serious circumstances could make him place dependence in a former rebel officer!"

Barry grinned, not at all happily. "You sound just the way you did when you told me that you'd never speak to me again."

Addison roused himself to put some authority into his voice. "Sergeant Barry is the ranking non-commissioned officer of United States forces on duty here, miss. I'm quite aware of his former status."

"Take it easy, Lieutenant," Barry advised. "Let her talk mad for a minute or so and then she'll remember that she's a nurse who's not supposed to disturb her patient."

Addison did not seem to have any strength left for another remark but Linda did. "I was honestly sorry when I heard that you had been killed, Tom," she said in a low voice. "But now I almost wish it had been true. You still have the nasty knack of being hateful!"

Barry chuckled. It seemed like old times. "Miss Conway and I are old friends," he told the wounded man. "Possibly you can detect the cordiality in her manner. But take it easy and she'll be a good nurse. There's a heart of gold behind that miserable disposition."

He wheeled his horse quickly and rode away. In a battle of words with Linda Conway, it was always well to leave before she could throw in her heavy artillery. There hadn't been many times in his life that he'd been able to do it.

The small glow of satisfaction didn't last long. Physical weariness was beginning to be overpowering and he found it difficult to concentrate on the various details that demanded his attention. He didn't even find time to ask himself why he should bother to assume responsibilities. All he knew was that there was a job that needed doing, a job that a lot of people were expecting him to do.

He found Wirtz preparing to send out flankers in the usual pattern so he simply said, "Take charge, Corporal. Better let Welland and Samuels ride a wagon for a while. We may need them a lot worse later."

"It leaves us mighty short-handed."

"I know. Sawdust can handle the point. You'd better take the rear. That way you can keep an eye on how things shape up."

"That's how I got it set. Strauss and Ladou are out on the flanks already."

"Good man. I'll stay with the wagons until I've got an idea how they're handling. Then I'll go up ahead with Sawdust. You'll have to keep an eye on everything."

Wirtz grinned crookedly. "Seems real funny that you're turnin' things over to me. Addison tell you to do it?"

"No. The Lieutenant's hurt pretty bad. Not serious, I guess, but bad enough so's he's not anywhere near as proddy as he was. He was mighty careful about letting me know he's calling me Sergeant again. While I'm running the job you're guard officer, and anything else we happen to need you for. Right?"

Wirtz grinned again, this time a little more cordially. "I reckon we'll git along all right, Sarge."

"No reason why not."

Wirtz started to turn away as though to take over his place at the rear of the column. Then he came back to ask, "You didn't forget about that other lot of Injun sign, did you? In this snow we might run smack into another war party. There's one out here, seems like."

It was Barry's turn to grin. "You're using your head, Corporal. Make sure they don't hit us from the rear."

The wagons were beginning to move steadily now and Barry rode slowly forward, taking note of how each wagon was loaded and where the wounded were being accommodated. Both Welland and Samuels were riding on wagon seats with the drivers and both offered their protests as he stopped to talk to them. He told them what he had told Wirtz about keeping them fit for future needs but it went through his mind that they had been relieved of active duty before he even suggested it to Wirtz. The corporal had been a step ahead of him on that point but had not bothered to say so. Maybe Wirtz was going to turn out all right.

Katie Hennessey was riding as nurse with the two wounded teamsters, her position as awkward as the one Linda Conway had assumed. She was cheerful about it, however, giving him a smile as he swung behind the wagon to look in.

"Do you think this snow will help us, Sergeant?" she inquired.

"For a while. I don't think it will amount to much, and maybe that's what we need. A little to cover our tracks and not enough to hold us up."

She smiled again, only her eyes showing the weariness and grief. "Make sure it happens that way," she replied. "Give the necessary orders."

He waved a hand in recognition of her small attempt at humor. Even a small attempt was good. While she could attempt a joke she wasn't going to break down.

He pulled up next beside the wagon driven by Abe Shingle. The train leader had become a driver in the emergency and Herbert Rossiter was riding at his side. Barry could read nothing in either man's face but he decided that he had better come to some sort of understanding with them. His own affairs—as he was beginning to guess— would take a lot more time to settle with Rossiter.

"Our scout is trying to find the shortest possible route back to the South Platte," he said abruptly. "It's our best chance of finding water."

"What the hell!" Shingle exploded. "That's where all the hell is bustin' out. We got away from there . . ."

"You didn't miss much by leaving it," Barry cut in briskly. "A wagon outfit can't hide from war parties. Water's more important than anything else now. We're going to push through."

"Gettin' damned officious, ain't you?" Shingle sneered.

"I've got my orders. You'll do well to let me carry them out."

To his surprise Rossiter broke in then. "The Sergeant knows his business, Abe. We'd better let him handle things as he sees fit."

"Thanks. Let me add that our scout tells me that there is no good trail west of here. We don't have any choice. Either we find the river or you lose your stock—and probably all our scalps."

"Get us through, Sergeant," Rossiter told him. "By this time you must know that you have an extra interest in the result. You and I will get together as soon as we have a chance."

Barry nodded and rode forward again until he could

swing in beside Jess Conway. "Rossiter began to sound peaceful a minute ago," he announced to the burly man. "Seems ready to admit that I've got some kind of a claim."

"He'd better!" Conway exclaimed. "He knows damned well that I'm fully aware of all the circumstances."

"Want to tell me? Briefly, that is. I'm too numb to put my mind on two things at a time and right now the big thing I've got to think about is Indians."

"Simple enough. Rossiter was in solid with the big politicians. He had some fat contracts and he needed your father's experience. I suppose he threw his weight into getting the payments through for the property the government had seized. With that extra capital from his new partner—your father, I mean—he could branch out in a big way. Then your father died and you were reported killed. Rossiter simply kept everything. A little later I made my deal with him, both of us figuring that the war would soon be over and that the big chance would be out here. It looks like we were in too much of a hurry."

"Thanks," Barry told him. "At least I know where I stand now." He rode on ahead of the wagon trying to decide just what he really meant by that remark. Maybe he knew more than he had known before but he still had a lot to learn about Rossiter. The man had certainly not acted like a fellow who intended doing the right thing by a partner.

He found Sawdust working out a winding passage through the broken country, the light powder of snow making it all the more difficult to judge grades and obstacles. "Sure of your direction?" Barry asked as he swung in beside the scout. "This snow could fool you."

"Not if the wind ain't changed. It was comin' outa the

nor-west and I ain't seen nothin' to make me think it changed."

"Likely you're right. Any chance that we could get snowbound?"

"It ain't likely. This here's kinda like them summer squalls only it's snow instead o' rain. We could run out of it anytime."

They rode in silence for some minutes but then Sawdust asked, "What's goin' on back there, Sarge? Seems like you kinda found ole friends."

"Maybe. Friends before the war, that is." He was thinking that there had been small show of friendship in the way Linda had talked to him.

"Is this here Conway the feller ye told me about? The one what was fixin' to set up partners with ye?"

"That's the man."

Sawdust chuckled. "And the gal. I seen her. Real purty."

"Forget about the girl. She's still of the opinion that I'm a traitor to the country. Anyway, it's pretty complicated now."

He told Sawdust what Conway had just explained to him. "I don't know how any part of it will work out. Property law is something I don't know too much about. I've got a claim, I suppose, but I don't know what chance I'd have of making it stand up in court. Nor is there much chance that I'd get to the proper court. Galvanized Yankees don't get furloughs to let them go east and start lawsuits."

"But Conway knows the way things stand and he's friendly. Right?"

"He seems to be. But forget it. We've got other problems right now."

"Mebbe we'd better shoot that polecat Rossiter. It would

settle things real neat."

"Sure. We could get hung for murder."

"What do ye figger to do?"

"About Rossiter? I'll wait a bit. For now it's enough to work out some way to get these wagons through to Denver. If I've got a claim on any part of this stuff it's a good claim. Flour's bringing forty-five dollars a barrel there. And about half of the load is flour."

Sawdust laughed. "Big business man already! Ye think Rossiter's figgerin' to let ye in on it?"

"Probably not. That's something I've got to work out when the time comes—if the Cheyennes don't settle it for us."

They rode in silence again, both of them weary enough so that even talking was a burden. Barry knew that Sawdust had not forgotten the Indian sign they had seen far to the north. That particular war party had gone farther west than the present path of the wagons. With the approach of cold weather they would be swinging back toward the winter villages in the east. There was still the risk of being cut off by them.

Barry found himself wondering whether the Indians were actually being incited by Confederate commissioners. He did not like the idea but he had to admit that the summer raids had extended well into a season when raids generally tapered off. During the three years that the Indians had been in a good position to wipe out every settlement and fort west of the Missouri they had done little about it. Now they were striking hard, continuing their raids past the raiding season. Either they had come to appreciate their opportunity or somebody was doing a lot of prodding.

His gloomy thoughts were interrupted by an exclamation from Sawdust. The scout was pointing to a creek ahead where brown water flowed. "Looks like there was a storm higher up," the scout said. "Got enough flowin' there so's stock kin drink."

"Take a look from that ridge," Barry suggested, pointing. "If the country ahead is clear we'll make a stop here. Some of that dead cottonwood along the bank will do for fires. A hot meal will help everybody."

He rode to another high point while Sawdust climbed the ridge. When neither of them could see any sign of hostiles in the surrounding country Barry went back to tell the drivers about the creek ahead. "We'll rest for an hour or so," he told Shingle. "Everybody needs the breather."

The lanky wagon boss nodded sullenly. "Mebbe we could push on into the night if we rest now. Less chance o' runnin' into Indians."

"And more chance of getting lost," Barry told him. "We'd better play it as safe as we can. Your extra stock is about gone, you know. With no spare animals for the teams we'll have to take it easy. No use pushing into the darkness when we'll only kill off the stock."

Rossiter spoke quickly, forestalling what appeared to be an angry comment from the station boss. "We'll do what the Sergeant thinks best. He's the man who knows this country."

Barry didn't bother to correct them. The only thing that concerned him was that he was not going to have any immediate quarrel about command. It didn't make any difference why Rossiter was siding with him. Getting into the

Rossiter problem was something that could be postponed.

He watched while the wagons moved in toward the stream. Shingle took charge and handled the watering with some show of skill. Some of the replacement drivers had trouble with their thirsty teams but Shingle took charge and handled everything. It was apparent that the man knew the freighting business even if he had not been particularly smart with regard to Indians.

After a few minutes Barry walked across to the wagon where Lieutenant Addison was trying to relax after the jolting ride. Linda Conway had left her patient while she went to speak with her parents.

"Feeling any better, Lieutenant?" Barry asked as he climbed up to look into the wagon.

"I wish I could say yes," Addison told him. "I just plain hurt all over. Where are we?"

"Right smack in the middle of nowhere. Sawdust thinks we might hit the South Platte by tomorrow but he's not sure. The only good part is that the snow seems to be easing a little."

"Any more Indian sign?"

"No, sir. We still figure that there's another war party in the area but we're hoping they've moved east along the river before we get there."

There was a pause before Addison said faintly, "Miss Conway told me about you, Sergeant. I begin to understand why Captain Pritchard thought well of you."

Barry let the crooked grin come. "I'm surprised. I didn't suppose Linda Conway would have said anything to make me look very good."

"She's angry. Hurt, maybe. But I don't think she hates

you as much as she pretends. Does that help any?"

Barry shook his head. "I'm not sure. A man gets used to being blamed for everything—when it happens often enough."

"I think I understand now." That seemed to exhaust the wounded man for he closed his eyes and said nothing more. Barry climbed down from the wagon and went directly across to the Conways.

It was Linda who turned to fire a prompt question at him. "Why are we stopped here? I should think we would drive just as hard as possible."

Barry repeated what he had told Shingle.

"Your orders, I suppose?" she snapped.

"My orders. I'm now responsible for wounded men. I'll get them through safely the best I can."

"I think you're taking a lot on yourself for a man who belongs in prison."

He gave her that lop-sided grin. "I've got the official documents to prove that I don't belong in prison. On the other hand, I'm beginning to think that some other smug folks I know ought to be there. If you want to take out your ill-humor on somebody go talk sassy to the man who disobeyed army orders and got some of our men killed."

"Careful," Conway warned in a low voice. "There's no point in stirring up extra trouble."

Barry nodded. "I'm sorry. Too tired to think straight, I guess." The grin came again as he added, "Melinda Jessie always did have the knack of making me talk too much."

"Melinda Jessie!" the girl exclaimed. "You know how I hate that name!"

"Sure. Now we're even." He felt a little better.

CHAPTER 10

"There's something I didn't tell you when we talked before," Conway said quickly, obviously trying to keep any petty argument down. "About the report of your death. It came only about a week after your father died. It occurs to me now that somebody might have done some tricks with the casualty lists."

"Meaning Rossiter?"

"It was a help to him."

"I'll keep it in mind."

Linda seemed to have lost some of her anger. "Do you really believe Mr. Rossiter tried to defraud you?"

"I don't know what to believe. I know that he seemed pretty sore at me when we first met. He tried to keep me from being assigned on this patrol. Now it seems possible that he had hoped to get down here to meet this wagon train without having to do business with a man he wanted to have on the dead list. How come he was out here ahead of you?"

"Much the same reason as your earlier trip," Conway told him. "He was to look things over and let us know. His letters pointed out the immediate opportunities and the probability that the war would soon end. So I put together a train and we started. Incidentally, all our eggs are not in the one basket. We still are partners in several bits of business back in the Ohio valley. Also we have another and larger train planned for a move west next spring. Possibly you have some claim to all of that."

"I'll be interested to hear how Rossiter is going to

explain things," Barry said in a low tone. "Don't say anything until he's had a chance."

They made good progress through the afternoon, running out of the real snowfall almost as soon as they left the muddy creek. A broken sky brought alternate sunshine and snow flurries but no one seemed to mind. The stock had been watered and the wagons were moving. Actually the animals were in better condition than the people of the train. During the little siege men had not dared to sleep but the horses had been idle, resting. Barry set a hard pace, trying to keep alert to the possible dangers ahead even though his eyes wanted to fall shut and his brain kept trying to work out answers to the Rossiter problem.

They found rougher travel in the late afternoon, the freshening northwest wind hinting at more snow as it drove clouds of biting dust into the faces of drivers and teams. Twice Sawdust and Barry almost led the train into impossible spots but each time they saw the difficulties in time to make the needed detour. Still they made less than a mile during the last two hours, the blowing sand obscuring the terrain until decent scouting became next to impossible. It was then that Barry decided to halt for the night. It would have to be a dry camp but that part was to be expected. The important matter was that they had suddenly moved into open country where attackers would have trouble in getting close undetected.

The wagons went into corral without waiting for orders. That much the teamsters had learned from their week of ordeal. How bad that week had been Barry did not learn until after he had taken care of his regular duties and had talked briefly with a slightly delirious Addison. Then

Conway sketched in the details. The wagons had left the still unfinished Fort Sedgwick against all advice, hopeful that the raiding farther east would not extend past the new military post. It hadn't taken them long to learn their mistake. A succession of burned fields, gutted cabins and unburied corpses told the story. No one had exaggerated when the warning had been passed that the Cheyennes were trying to wipe out every white along the Platte.

On the second day they had interrupted the attack on a single wagon and had picked up Katie Hennessey. She had been holding off a small war party, her husband and a hired wagon driver dead beside her. Her explanation of why the three of them had been coming east into the ravaged country had not been very logical but no one had pressed the matter. They had simply taken her with them, leaving her only time to salvage her personal belongings while the wagoners buried the two dead men.

Two other refugees joined them the next morning, both farmers who had escaped Indian attacks farther south. It turned out that the extra hands were useful enough because one day later the real fighting began. At first there had been only hit-run attacks by small parties but evidently the word had been passed and the Indian attackers grew in numbers. The wagons fought a retreating action, hopeful of reaching help although it seemed certain that there would be greater dangers ahead. The refugees helped in the fighting and Mrs. Hennessey showed her mettle in caring for the wounded.

It was at that point that Shingle ordered the crossing of the river. He claimed that the only hope of avoiding other war parties was to detour. His idea was that the harrying raids were merely a device for driving the train into a fatal ambush which was being prepared by larger forces of Cheyennes in the west. Accordingly he claimed that the way to avoid trouble was to by-pass the spot where the ambushers waited.

"Seems like the man never had much experience fighting Indians," Barry commented dryly.

"He didn't. Good wagon man, I'd say, but he learned his trade back in Illinois."

Barry nodded. "He didn't have much chance at that. Not only was there a war party along the river ahead of you but the other hostiles must have passed the word to friends farther north. We hit their trail and followed them to you. They seemed to know exactly where they were going."

"Lucky you arrived when you did. I thought they'd finish us off last night but somehow they couldn't seem to make up their minds to attack."

"Just another Indian weakness," Barry told him. "They like the early morning for their big moves. And Sawdust has a notion that there was some kind of rivalry afoot between the chiefs. Anyway they didn't make their move. Now we've got to do some guessing about how they'll take their licking. If they're hurt bad enough maybe we'll get through to the Colorado patrols before they can rally around."

The early evening was routine. Shingle and Rossiter made no attempt to interfere with Wirtz's posting of guards, even lending a hand to see that wagoners and refugees took a turn at the duty. No one had much to say. Everyone was bordering on complete exhaustion but they prepared for the night with grim care, well aware that they were still a long way from safety.

Barry took charge of the first guard detail, anxious to make sure that the more exhausted men didn't draw the early assignments. He wanted men on the first shift who could keep awake until the others could snatch a bit of sleep.

The camp was silent when he came in from his first inspection of guards, only Herbert Rossiter appearing wakeful. The stout man had hunched himself in a blanket beside the dying fire of buffalo chips and Barry knew a quick feeling that the man was waiting for him. It seemed like as good a time as any to get some talking done.

Rossiter looked up as he limped toward the fire, his greeting almost casual. "Think we'll get through, Sergeant?" he asked.

"The odds are getting better. Those militia patrols can't be more than a couple of days ahead."

"You've been right most of the time. I hope you're still that way."

Barry sat down without showing his surprise. Actually he wasn't completely astonished at the new approach. Suspicion had warned him that Rossiter might take such a tack. "I depend on Featherstone," he said shortly. "He's the one who needs to be right."

"No matter. I've been pretty harsh toward you. Maybe bitter is the word I ought to use. I suppose you know why?"

"Because I stand in your way?"

"Of course not!" The man seemed honestly disturbed. "It was because I didn't believe you. I thought you were an imposter."

This time Barry let his surprise show. "How do you mean that?"

"I'd think it would be quite clear. I came out here believing that you were dead. I now hold title to property that is partly yours—only I didn't know it. Then I ran across a man who called himself Tom Barry. I began to suspect that someone was trying to work out a scheme to claim the property of a dead man. Naturally I didn't propose to let that happen."

Barry didn't believe a word of it but he was not going to argue the matter just yet. He wanted to know how Rossiter was planning his campaign. "Want to tell me about the whole deal?" he asked quietly.

"Not too much to tell. Anyway, I think Conway must have explained most of it. Shortly after you were taken prisoner I made a deal with your father. He had a claim but was in no position to do much about it. I had influence. I used that influence to get his claim paid and we went into partnership with the proceeds. In that way your father's dubious status as a rebel was not a complicating factor. It worked out quite well. Our joint efforts were reasonably profitable.

"Then we began to look forward to the end of the war and the chances that a man might find here in the west. Unfortunately, your father contracted pneumonia just then and died. I tried to trace you, hoping that you would agree to continue the partnership with me. About six months passed and then you were listed as having been killed in an Indian fight near Green River. I could find no other claimant to your father's property so I claimed it as a surviving partner. Perfectly legal, you understand."

"Of course."

"So I operated in my own name and after a time formed

a new partnership with Jess Conway. Your father had often talked of taking him into our plans. It seemed like a good deal all around. The whole trouble was that your friends down south wouldn't admit that they were beaten. They refused to surrender and now they're raising the Indians against us! Our first try at grabbing a piece of the western trade is turning out to be rough."

Barry let the silence come between them. Rossiter was talking desperately and Barry had no intention of easing the situation for him. He still did not trust the man so it seemed like a good idea to let him talk. Maybe his glibness would begin to slip a little.

Finally Rossiter jerked both hands out in a nervous motion. "So I made some mistakes!" he snapped. "I was plenty worried when I heard that our wagons might run into these Indian raids. It didn't make me feel any better when the army sent the stagecoach so far north. Then I ran headlong into a man who called himself Tom Barry. You can imagine how I felt."

He broke off again but went on in an easier tone, "However, the Conways assure me that you are really the Tom Barry I believed to be dead. Naturally you have a claim on much of the property I have been treating as my own. It will take time to work out the details but I don't believe you will be in any hurry. The army isn't likely to turn you loose until the war is finally over. Meanwhile rest assured that I'm not trying to defraud you of anything."

"I'm a lot more worried about what the Cheyennes might try to do to me," Barry said in a low tone. He wished that he could be more alert. Rossiter made it all sound pretty reasonable. A man who was too tired to think had no business listening to smooth talk.

"So we understand each other," Rossiter told him. "Now get some sleep. I thought maybe you'd rest easier if we settled this misunderstanding between us."

"Thanks. Sleep is what I need."

He had a few minutes to puzzle over the talk before Wirtz relieved him as guard officer. The effort didn't turn out well. He wasn't sure that he was thinking straight but in a weary sort of way he knew that Rossiter might have told the exact truth. Just as certainly the story was the kind of thing that would be told by a man who was a thorough scoundrel.

With the wind blowing cold out of the northwest he looked around for a decent place to get some sleep. The only sheltered spot which did not seem to be occupied was a little cranny where some temporarily unloaded boxes were stacked against the side of a wagon. He was crawling under with his blanket across his shoulder when a calm voice asked, "Are you planning to move in, Sergeant?"

He recognized Mrs. Hennessey's voice. "Sorry. I didn't know anybody was here."

"No matter. There's room. Another blanket will help."

He still hadn't moved since she had first spoken. When he continued to hesitate she gave a shaky little laugh. "Don't worry, Sergeant. I'm not interested in what anyone will say or think. At the moment I'm more concerned about not being able to keep warm."

He chuckled to himself as he crawled forward, thinking about how foolish convention could be and how a man remembered such things at ridiculous times. "Suits me fine," he assured her.

Groping in the darkness he found where she had huddled

against the stack of boxes. "Pull my blanket around you," he ordered. "I'll take the part that's left over. I'm already wearing an overcoat, you know."

She busied herself while he waited on hands and knees. Then she murmured, "Roll in beside me. I think we'll do all right."

He followed instructions and she slipped the blanket around him. He let his body press against her, oddly amused that she was no more than a bulky weight to the touch. Evidently she must have sensed some of his amusement for she said softly, "Scarcely the conduct to be expected of a recent widow. Somehow I don't feel any particular shame."

He wasn't quite sure what to say in return so he didn't say anything. Before he could come up with any kind of remark he was sound asleep.

When he awoke again it was to the knowledge that he was aching in a lot of places. He had a confused feeling that something was happening in the wagon camp but he couldn't get his wits together to figure it out. And he couldn't see. When he tried to move he couldn't manage it, the drugged weariness of sleep preventing him from understanding why he was so helpless.

Then his brain began to clear a little and he knew that his right arm was pinned down. After that he figured things out readily enough. Somehow he had managed to roll around during the night and had taken the blanket swathed form of Mrs. Hennessey into his arms. His own blanket now covered both of them and had been pulled up over their heads.

He got his free hand working and pulled the blanket down a little, discovering then that he had the woman's hair in his eyes. By that time she stirred a little and asked, "Is it time to get started?"

Before he could reply she uttered a funny little grunt as though realizing the situation. He pulled his cramped arm out from under her and began to roll clear. "At least we kept warm," he said.

That was when another voice broke in. "Lieutenant Addison would like to see you before we start the day's march. I know he'll be happy that you spent such a comfortable night."

Barry lay still after one complete roll that took him out of the blanket. He was flat on his back under the edge of the wagon, looking up at Linda Conway in the gray of a murky dawn. He could not see her expression in the half light but her tone was eloquent enough. For a moment all he could think about was that Addison had certainly picked a fine time to send out Linda as his messenger.

She was gone before he could find his tongue so he simply rolled again and came to his knees beyond the wagon wheel. Mrs. Hennessey followed, trailing his blanket but still wrapped in her own. "I take it that you're in trouble," she said briefly.

"I'm always in trouble."

"But not this kind."

He took the blanket from her and climbed to his feet, trying to work some circulation into the cramped right arm. "Forget it. Just name a kind of trouble. I'll find it!"

He moved away without letting her say anything more. It was nearly dawn. The other men had let him sleep through the night. Now he had to get down to business. Maybe he could forget Linda's tone if he made himself busy enough.

Chapter 11

There was little that needed his attention. Wirtz and Sawdust had doubled the last shift of guards, alert against the possibility of a dawn attack, but the scouts soon learned that no hostiles had approached during the night. A hasty breakfast was consumed in relays, the air of tension and worry obvious all around in spite of the fact that men were taking care of their duties with a good show of efficiency. Shingle was getting the train organized, seeing to it that the wounded were made as comfortable as possible. Barry delayed a little while before going across to see Addison, trying to let some of his angry embarrassment subside.

He found the wounded officer in reasonably good spirits, having spent a comfortable night with the trace of fever leaving him. "Give me another day," Addison boasted weakly, "and I'll be able to relieve you of routine duties. Meanwhile you're on your own."

They talked for a few moments about the trail ahead and the risk of further Indian attacks. Then Linda Conway came to stand at the back of the wagon. She had washed her face and tidied her hair a bit so that she looked mighty good to Barry. She didn't even sound angry when she asked, "Will you try to avoid as much of the rough country as possible today, Sergeant? Lieutenant Addison's wounds have a tendency to bleed when he's jolted around. Mrs. Hennessey tells me that the same is true of one of the drivers she is attending."

The impersonal way she said it was almost as bad as anger. Barry looked her squarely in the eyes for a split second but then nodded. "We'll do what we can," he assured her. "Once we get across to the South Platte we ought to find things a bit smoother."

She ignored him rather pointedly then, climbing into the wagon to ride with her patient. Barry saw that the first wagons were already moving so he swung into the saddle and passed some final warnings to his men. "Look sharp today, boys. There's going to be plenty of dust blowing and it'll be hard to tell about what you're seeing. Don't raise any false alarms but don't take chances. The wagons will need all the warning they can get if hostiles show up."

"We'll be ready," Wirtz told him grimly. "Ain't none of us that don't know how sore them varmints is goin' to be after what we done to 'em. They'll be back as soon as they can pick up some help."

"And don't forget that there's likely to be other bands out ahead of us."

"We'll handle 'em," Samuels told him. The man was still sticking close to the wagons but his wound wasn't bothering him enough to keep him out of the saddle.

Barry felt a little easier when he rode forward to join Sawdust. Those men on the flanks knew what they were doing. They'd fought the Cheyennes and had beaten them; they were confident that they could do it again.

The sun was already beginning to take some of the chill out of the November morning when he pulled up to ride beside Featherstone. The scout was staying a good quarter of a mile ahead of the wagons and keeping to the high ground as much as possible. He answered Barry's opening question with a grunt of disgust.

"Can't tell a damned thing about it. Dust blowin' everywhere. Reminds me of a tale old Jim Bridger useta tell about a sandstorm that got so bad that they found a gopher diggin' a tunnel ten feet offa the ground."

Barry laughed. Evidently Sawdust had gotten enough sleep to be feeling like himself again. "No sign of hostiles?"

"Nope. And that's the hell of it. Ole Jim useta say that when ye can't see no Injuns that's the time to be scairt of 'em."

"How much farther to the river?"

"Mebbe four—five hours. Not that we're goin' to be in any healthier country when we git there. I ain't forgot that other lot o' sign we seen."

They rode silently for a mile or so but then Sawdust remarked with elaborate casualness, "Right peert last night. Mighty handy to have somebody to git cozy with."

"You go to hell," Barry told him in the same casual tone.

Sawdust laughed. "I hunted all over hell for ye when it was time fer the dawn shift. Then I found ye and didn't have the heart to bust up a good thing. Seems like the widder musta been easy to console."

"She was cold."

"I'll bet she could warm up real good."

"I didn't find out." He grinned a little more easily as he added, "A man kinda gets his style cramped when he wears his overcoat to bed."

"Ye didn't!"

"I did. So forget it."

"The Conway gal won't. I seen her face when she woke ye. I still think that gal's got a soft spot fer ye. Leastways she did before this mornin'."

"Go to hell," Barry repeated. This time he didn't make it sound casual.

The dust subsided a little by midmorning, the gradual flattening of the land hinting that they had worked their way out of the worst of the rock country. Barry began to feel a little easier. Water would not be too far ahead. There had been no sign of Cheyennes. For the moment it was enough to cheer about. He preferred not to think about more personal matters.

There was a brief halt at noon, no fires being lighted. Weary people munched on hard rations and let their teams rest. Then they moved on again, trying to whittle away the miles and waiting for the dangers which all of them expected to find along the river.

For Barry the next few hours were an ordeal. He was having to stare into the afternoon sun with eyes that still smarted from scant sleep. And there was nothing but dullness in the route, nothing to keep him from worrying about Rossiter and Shingle. Nothing, that is, except a recurring annoyance every time his mind turned to Linda Conway.

Two hours before sunset they eased down a long slope toward the almost bare channel of the South Platte. The flankers covered the move with extra care but nothing happened. When the teamsters paused to water their horses and to fill the water barrels Barry and Sawdust went across to scout the far side of the river. There they found enough Indian sign to keep them busy for quite a while. It was hard to read, the blowing sand having covered much of it, but it was clear enough that two large parties of warriors had ridden downstream not long before.

"Could be bad," Barry muttered. "If those hellions we

beat off meet up with either of these bands they'll turn back and give us a real bad time."

"Likely one o' these parties is the one we know rode down outa the north. If that's right we don't have to figure on 'em bein' ahead of us."

Barry pulled a crooked grin. "I'm glad you can find something cheerful about it. Let's get those wagons across. From here on we're making a bit of a run for it."

He rode back across the stream to tell the others what the sign indicated. Abe Shingle promptly tried to take charge. "I say we stick to this side and make all the miles we can," the wagon boss snapped. "No point in wastin' time with a crossin' now. It'll just give them bastards more of a chance to double back on us."

"Two reasons why you're wrong," Barry told him. "The easy trail is on the other side. We'll make better progress when we get on it. And this is an easy crossing. We'd be in a fix if we had to make a crossing with the Cheyennes pressing us. Better cross here and get ready for the worst."

"Is that the army talkin'?" Shingle demanded.

"Let's say so."

Suddenly the lanky man grinned. "You're the boss. I'll pass the word."

Barry was left with the feeling that he didn't like to win a point this way. Shingle wasn't the kind to give in so easily.

There was no delay in making the crossing. The sand was firm and the water low. The wagons went over smoothly and within the hour the train was moving again along the rutted trail which edged the south bank of the river. By that time Sawdust had ridden a wide circle and discovered more Indian sign at a little distance from the river trail. His guess was that scouts had accompanied the larger parties. At any rate the Indians had been headed east, presumably on their way to winter villages along Sand Creek, the Arickaree, or the Republican.

"Let's hope the snow chases them fast," Barry said glumly. "I'm afraid it won't work that way."

After a few minutes he dropped back to ride with the rear guard. That was where the danger would be now. There was still a chance that other bands of hostiles were ahead of the train but the chance seemed to be a small one. Certainly it was not as big a danger as the one he had already discussed with Sawdust. The defeated Indians would certainly try to return with one of those war parties if they happened to meet them. And there was a strong probability that they would.

Still everything was quiet when they went into corral for the night, picking a spot where the river had some clear pools in it. Conserving water was always good business, even when the casks were full. It was a silent camp. The wagoners were not as exhausted as they had been on the previous night but reaction was setting in. Together with the tension it made them morose, almost sullen. Men went about their chores doggedly, almost as though walking in their sleep. The women left their nursing duties only to get food. Such cooking as was done was in the hands of a bewhiskered little man who worked in silence, paying no attention to the grumbling that he seemed to expect. Barry almost hoped that more hostiles would show up. Danger instead of mere continuing strain might make everybody feel a little better.

The only bright spot was the fact that Addison seemed a great deal better but still in his new mood of comparative mellowness. He found Linda performing nurse's duties, having propped the wounded man up against a feed sack so that she could spoon some kind of broth into him. Mrs. Conway had taken pains to prepare the food for the wounded men. Now Linda and Katie Hennessey were taking care of the patients. It occurred to Barry that the routine was becoming reasonably efficient.

"Evening, Lieutenant," Barry greeted. "Seems like there's not much to report. No Indian sign since the river crossing."

Linda did not look around. She paused with her spoon held in midair while Addison replied, "Excellent. You're doing a fine piece of work for all of us, Sergeant."

It seemed to Barry that some of the pompousness was back in the Lieutenant's voice so he said crisply, "Yes, sir. Thank you, sir."

Addison laughed. "Stop it! I didn't mean to sound stuffy—although I suppose you've come to expect it of me. Drop the formalities." He obviously intended to add something to that but had to swallow broth or duck. Linda was getting rather definite in her efforts to spoon the stuff into him.

"Better eat now, Lieutenant," Barry advised as he sized up the situation. "Melinda Jessie is a woman of strong will. She wants you to eat and she's not keen on having you talk to a reprobate like me. So you'd better eat. That soup won't look good on your blouse."

"I am Miss Conway to you," the girl snapped. "You will please omit any future attempts at misguided humor. Men who deny their country have no excuse to be humorous!"

Addison frowned at her outburst. "Miss Conway!" he protested. "In all fairness let's admit that Sergeant Barry has been serving his country—and us—rather well in the past few days."

She put the dipper on a flattened flour sack and scrambled inelegantly toward the back opening of the wagon. "Admit what you please, sir!" she retorted. "If you think he's so wonderful . . . let him feed you!"

The haughty tone lost much of its effectiveness when she slid out of the wagon and had the bottom of her skirt catch on the tail gate. The result was that she slid to the ground with her skirt yanked to her shoulders. Barry needed to take only a step and then he lifted her while he reached out to free the snagged garment. He used rather more force than was necessary in dusting down her skirts and while he had her firmly held he murmured, "The weather's turning cold, Melinda Jessie. You'd better start wearing more underneath."

She fled without a reply, almost running. Barry watched her go but then he climbed into the wagon. "I guess she called my hand, Lieutenant. I'll be nurse."

"You don't need to, Sergeant. I have one good hand. I can manage."

Barry persisted and presently Addison broke in between swallows. "I can't get over Miss Conway's outburst. She talked a lot about you as we rolled along today. My impression was that she once thought a great deal of you and might feel the same way again. Now the pair of you . . ." He didn't need to finish.

"Linda's a funny sort of girl," Barry told him seriously.

"She's smart about a lot of things—like deciding to be a Unionist—but sometimes it's hard for her to see the other fellow's side. I suppose she'll never forgive me for being a Confederate soldier."

"And that bothers you?" Addison was being rather sharp about it.

"Not particularly. I can't live with the past, you know. If she wants to hate me over a thing like that I can't do much about it."

"I wanted to know," the lieutenant told him. "If you no longer have any intentions toward Miss Conway . . ." Again he let the thought trail away unsaid. Barry didn't help him out. He wasn't sure what he ought to say—if anything.

He finished with his new duty and slid down out of the wagon, a quick grin coming to his lips as he remembered what had happened to Linda when she tried the same move. It was then that Addison remarked, "You ought to know that I had an unexpected visitor today, Sergeant. Mr. Rossiter came over to apologize for his break of the other morning."

"No!" Barry turned to stare into the now dark interior of the wagon. "Did he try to explain his actions?"

"Yes. He said his horse bolted. I didn't try to make a point of it. Actually, I don't suppose it made any difference. We were going into a real trap anyway." There was just a tinge of bitterness in the final words.

"Watch him," Barry warned. "I think the man is up to something. I thought it involved me personally but now I'm not sure."

"He spoke well of you," Addison said. "Suggested that I

mention you favorably in whatever report I make. Which I propose to do, of course."

"Thanks, but don't let him fool you. There's something brewing behind that fat face. I'm sure of it."

He wasn't thinking about Rossiter as he moved away from the wagon. A curious mixture of amusement and annoyance pushed Rossiter into the background of his emotions. The amusement was in memory of how he had spent the past few minutes with Lieutenant Addison. He wondered what Captain Pritchard would have said if he could have seen the severe young officer being fed by a Galvanized Yankee and talking to him on friendly terms. That was the amusing part. What Addison had suggested about his own interest in Linda Conway was not so amusing.

It became even less a matter of amusement when he found himself confronted by the young lady's mother a moment or so later. Mrs. Conway made certain that they were out of earshot of the others before she asked, "What in the world did you say to Linda, Tom? She came to our wagon practically in tears. They were angry tears but still tears."

"I called her Melinda Jessie, for one thing. That generally stirs up a bit of argument. And she seemed to think that there was something illegal about the Lieutenant telling me I had done a good job."

"No more than that?"

"Mrs. Conway, you know how it was with Linda and me. When we broke off it was pretty bad. I don't think she ever got completely over being mad and hurt that I didn't agree with her."

"And I don't think she ever got over being in love with you, Tom."

Barry stared in the darkness. His relationship with the woman he had expected to have as a mother-in-law had always been completely cordial but she had never done anything to promote the romance between her daughter and himself. Now she sounded like other mothers he had known.

Evidently she realized it for she went on quickly, "I know what you must think. Please try to understand. If you and Linda want to forget the past it's none of my business. But I don't want you to continue quarreling with each other simply because neither of you understand how the other feels."

"I'm sorry, ma'am," Barry said quietly, still trying to figure out why the woman had come to him. "Maybe I'm just keeping my guard up."

"What do you mean by that?"

"I'm not so sure. All I know is that I've been trying to do what I promised to do when I switched uniforms but all the time people distrust me and remind me that I'm some kind of a traitor. I know those things happen in war time but it still hurts. After a year of getting it from most of the officers I began to build up a sort of mental callous against it. I keep on doing what I think is my duty and not giving a damn what anybody says." He didn't think it wise to add that he also had played hob with a lot of stuffy regulations as a sort of revolt against authority.

"And Linda keeps reminding you of your position? Is that it?"

"I reckon so."

"Didn't it ever occur to you that perhaps she had raised a few callouses of her own during the past three or four years? It wasn't easy for her to have you walk out on her. It wasn't easy for her to explain to friends that the man she had intended to marry had chosen to leave her for a cause she hated."

"I guess I can see the point," Barry said shortly. "Are you hinting that she's not as sore as she sounds?"

"I don't know. But I don't think her tears were pure anger."

"Thanks. I'll see what I can do about it."

Mrs. Conway slipped away in the darkness and Barry went across to a fire where several of his men were laughing about something. He had almost reached them when a woman's voice sounded. Katie Hennessey was apparently the center of attraction in the circle.

"But I'm not Irish at all," the blonde woman was telling somebody. "I simply married Hennessey. My name became Katie then but it's really Kaatje. I'm Dutch."

Barry changed his mind about joining the group. He wasn't sure what kind of callouses Katie Hennessey was building for herself but he had a hunch that she wasn't intending to remain a widow very long. He decided that tonight he wasn't going to share his blanket.

CHAPTER 12

The night passed quietly. The wind had died out, making the cold easier to take, but when they turned out a little before dawn there was frost on the ground, on the wagon tops, and on the blankets of those who had slept in the open. The whiskery cook suddenly had more helpers than he could use. His fire was the only one in camp.

When the pickets reported the prairie clear of enemies Barry passed the word to Shingle and the wagon boss did his usual good job of getting the train into motion. Barry rode out ahead with Sawdust long enough to make certain that the trail was clear ahead of them. Then the two men climbed to the highest ground handy and stared hard into the east. It wasn't so important that the frosty ruts ahead were clear of enemies; what counted was the threat in the rear. And now was the time to look hard. When the sun began to come up above that frost there would be a blind period.

They moved from one vantage point to another, and then had to give up as the sun hit them squarely in the eyes. By that time Barry was satisfied. "No war party real close," he growled. "I'll drop back now. You stick with the high ground as much as possible. Don't risk getting into anything but range a bit wide. The trails on both sides of the river are open enough so you won't need to do more than take a look once in a while."

"I'm goin' to git lonesome up here," Sawdust complained. "Long as ye ain't sparkin' the widder woman no more how'd it be to send her up here to ride with me. I ain't sech a bad sort of feller."

"Not such a bad sort of feller," Barry repeated. "Just an idiot who thinks he's funny when he's not. Anyway Mrs. Hennessey is nursing wounded men."

"I could cut my throat," Sawdust proposed solemnly.

"You do that." He turned back toward the wagons, a little pleased at having something to chuckle over. For a man who enjoyed good humor the past three years hadn't been much to brag about. Quizzically he wondered whether anybody else had ever been responsible for fighting Indians while having so many other things to think about. It was pretty difficult to keep his mind on Indians when all the time there were problems involving women, property, politics, prejudices and a dozen other things.

The sun was warming things up nicely when he swung in beside Gerhardt Strauss for an exchange of comments. Ladou had already reported no sign of Indians and now Strauss backed him up on it. The land to the south was bare. As nearly as they could tell the more broken country beyond the river was equally empty.

Suddenly he saw that Corporal Wirtz was waving some sort of signal from the rear. The big militiaman had halted at the top of a rise and was looking back down the river.

"Look alive," he told Strauss. "This could be it." Then he was riding back to the spot where Wirtz was waiting.

The corporal simply pointed as Barry came up. It was easier to look into the east now, the sun high enough so that it was no longer blinding. There was a swirl of dust there. Nothing really definite but dust at a time when no wind was kicking it up.

"I thought I seen riders just before I waved to you," Wirtz told him. "Now there ain't nothin' but that blurry spot."

Barry judged that the bit of haze was some two to three miles behind the wagons. It would take quite a lot of dust to show so plainly at that distance and from behind a low ridge. He was fairly certain that they were seeing only the top of it.

"Likely you saw somebody on the high ground beyond,"

he murmured. "Now they're out of sight between ridges. Good eyes, Corporal."

"Sawdust claimed there was forty-fifty bastards in that war party," Wirtz remarked. "I figger it would take that many to raise so much dust."

"Could be. I suppose our friends of the other morning picked up some of the gang that was raiding west of here. We had to expect it."

They waited for a few minutes but then Barry nodded toward the wagons that had been drawing farther away from them. "We'll keep an eye on the rear but we'd better not get too far away. This could be a trick to get our attention while another outfit slips in from one side or the other. We saw the sign of two parties, you'll remember."

He left Wirtz long enough to overtake the wagons and send Samuels out with the warning to the other out-riders. After that a good two hours passed before the dust appeared as anything but a vague blur. Barry made sure that they did not lag too far behind the wagons but that made it difficult to pick good observation posts and hold them. The dust always seemed to be rising from behind some bit of high ground. Finally the suspense ended. Twelve warriors could be seen and counted. They came on in single file across the summit of a ridge.

"Either we guessed wrong about how many it takes to raise dust or there's more of them angling off to hit us from the side. I'll send Samuels back to join you. He's itching to be a little more active."

This time he made contact with each of his men as well as with the wagoners, letting them know what was happening and what might be expected in the way of possible flank attack. "I don't think they'll hit us today," he told them. "But we've got to stay ready. My guess is that they're trying to draw our attention to the rear and set up a big attack from another angle early tomorrow morning."

To the flankers he added a specific order. "Fire a gun if you see any sign of movement other than in the rear. Give the wagons as much time to corral as possible."

Addison asked only one question. "Is it possible that the dozen on our trail are the only ones chasing us?"

"Possible, I suppose. But why? They know we're tough so why should they try to jump us with a small party when they must have another hundred warriors not far away?"

The Lieutenant smiled faintly. "That's something you'll have to figure out for yourself, Sergeant. I only asked." He was propped up so that he could look out of the back of the wagon and watch the distant dust plume.

Linda Conway had been sitting beside him almost without moving while Barry reported. Now she asked in a calm voice, "Could these Indians be the same ones who attacked us before? Perhaps some of the survivors got their nerve back and want to try again."

"Again it's possible," Barry told her soberly. "It's always hard to tell what an Indian will do. I still figure those survivors have had a chance to meet up with the war parties we've talked about."

"Use your best judgment, Sergeant," Addison said. "You've been doing mighty well so far."

Somehow Barry didn't feel too good about it as he rode away. For some reason Linda had been courteous without being friendly. And she had been riding with her patient although it seemed clear that Addison was in no particular need of care. He wondered whether the officer's remark of the previous evening had been a really serious one. Not that he could blame the man for taking an interest in Linda. The girl was certainly attractive.

He pushed the thought away from him—or tried to. Thinking about Linda Conway was something he could not afford at the moment.

Minutes later he pulled up beside Sawdust to let him know what had been happening at the rear. The scout had no suggestions to offer. There had been no new Indian sign along the trail and no hint of trouble anywhere in the rolling country ahead. It didn't seem possible that any substantial party of horsemen could be moving anywhere within miles without making dust that would be visible.

"Nothin' ahead that looks like a spot fer an ambush," Sawdust told him. "If they're plannin' to hit us we'll know about it in time. Seems like a damned funny kind of Injun move."

"I still don't like it."

"Cheer up, Sarge. Ye're jest worryin' too much when it ain't supposed to be your job to do any of the worryin' at all. If'n any Injuns try to jump us now we'll fix 'em like the feller ole Jim Bridger useta tell about. Seems this varmint tried to steal a hoss right out of a camp full o' trappers what knew their shootin' plenty good. They blasted him so hard that instead o' buryin' him they took him to the assayer. He proved out thirty per cent lead."

Barry laughed, knowing that Sawdust was trying to make him feel better. Then he swung in a wide circle to ride the ridge while the wagons rolled past him. Still he could see no sign of life except for the twelve warriors down the river. He joined Wirtz and Samuels when the pair came along, noting that the Indians were now only about a mile in the rear.

"They act mighty odd," Samuels told him. "They was comin' up fast when I first got a good look at 'em but lately they're holdin' their distance. Just trailin' along almost peaceful like."

Wirtz nodded his agreement. "Any sign of militia patrols ahead of us?"

"No. I'd guess that they're steering clear of those big war parties that were out that way. Maybe they don't know that the Indians have headed east."

Samuels grinned. "Might as well look at it cheerful. It could be that the war parties left because the militia was botherin' 'em. Mebbe we're gittin' close to a few friends fer a change."

"I'd feel better if we could get rid of those friends we've got on our tails."

The puzzle went unanswered as the day wore along. What bothered Barry as much as anything was the way the teamsters were showing nerves again. They had fought their way through the worst of the danger area and had done a mighty good job of it. Now the uncertainty and the constant tension was getting to them. It didn't seem to make any difference to them that they outnumbered the visible enemy; they were simply getting edgy enough so that they didn't think straight. Drivers lashed their teams when there was no possible point in it. Rifles had appeared on wagon seats as though men expected to need them at a second's notice. The women were just as tense. Mrs. Conway carried a rifle across her lap and Katie Hennessey was walking beside her wagon, keeping a nervous eye on the rear. Only Linda Conway seemed unaffected and Barry understood why when he passed by the wagon. The girl was writing something at Lieutenant Addison's dictation.

Addison hailed him with a happy smile. "Not many junior officers get clerical help, Sergeant. Miss Conway is helping me to put my report in writing while I can still keep most of the facts in mind."

Barry nodded. "Not too easy to write in a jolting wagon."

"I'll manage," Linda said without even looking up. Barry would have felt better about it if she'd shown at least a little annoyance toward him.

He was so lost in his own glum thoughts that he was as startled as anyone else when Ladou's carbine barked a warning from the south flank. He spurred his horse around to race for the spot, vaguely aware that teamsters were shouting wildly at each other. It was only when he was clear of the wagons that he realized what some of the shouts had been like. At least two voices had yelled predictions that this time the savages would be backed by rebel guerrillas. For the first time in several hours he was being reminded that a lot of people were still in deadly fear of what this mysterious plot might turn out to be.

He turned back quickly, bawling orders for the wagons to go into corral. Somehow he made them listen to him, Abe Shingle turning the reins over to Rossiter and lending a hand at organization. Barry waited just long enough to be sure that the moment of panic was over, then he spurred on up the slope to where Ladou was making frantic motions toward him.

By the time he was in a position to see beyond the ridge

he could also see that the Cajun was red under his deep tan. The man sputtered in a mixture of English and bayou French, finally getting across the idea that he had made a mistake. He had seen dust in the distance and had fired his warning, almost immediately realizing that the dust had been raised by a herd of buffalo.

"Don't worry about it," Barry soothed. "I told you to warn first and ask questions later. Maybe it was a good jolt for the folks on the wagons."

When he went back to explain he was met by a mixture of relief and anger. These people had been scared too long to relish any kind of extra jolt. Even relief at finding that they were not in immediate danger didn't make them feel much better.

"What kind of Goddam lunatics have you got in that bob-tail army of yours?" Shingle snarled. "Can't that stupid rebel tell a Cheyenne from a buffalo?"

"He had his orders," Barry retorted. "He carried them out. Rather a false alarm than no alarm at all."

"Stupid damned fool! Now everybody's got to . . ."

"Stop bellyaching! It'll be just as well if we stop here for the night. The way your men have been lashing their horses we won't have any stock left for tomorrow."

"Don't tell me how to run my train, Mister Galvanized Yankee! We drive hard because there ain't no other choice."

"You've got no choice now!" Barry told him shortly. "We halt here. That's an order!"

"Whose order?"

"Mine. And don't try to buck it!"

His tone seemed to make Shingle hesitate. Barry took

quick advantage. "All of these people need rest. Everybody's jumpy. You're driving your teams and yourselves too hard just because the strain is getting you down. You're imagining things. When I rode away from here a little while ago I heard men yelling ridiculous things about rebel troops being with the Indians. That's wild imagination! I'll warrant that there's not a Confederate soldier between here and the Texas border except us damned Galvanized Yankees." He let a wry smile come with the final phrase and knew that he had impressed them. Already some of them were beginning to look ashamed of themselves.

Suddenly Rossiter gave him unexpected assistance. "He's right, folks," the man declared loudly. "We ought to know by this time that we can't force stock too far. I think we'd better trust Sergeant Barry. He hasn't made any mistakes yet."

Abe Shingle looked completely confused. Then he took his cue and muttered something that sounded like agreement. Barry plunged ahead, knowing that safety for everyone depended upon keeping down the threat of panic. These men could fight well enough; he had to make them believe in themselves.

"Settle down, all of you," he directed. "Take time to get your wits together. Meanwhile I'll take a patrol out and make sure that we don't have other hostiles around. Maybe we'll even make a few passes at those hellions behind us. I'm curious to see how they'll act if we show them we're not much scared of 'em."

"We're still wastin' good daylight," Shingle growled.

"And maybe saving horses. Talk some sense into him, Mr. Rossiter."

He turned away without getting a reply. It was the right time to go. There had been enough talk. The big scare was over.

He stopped to tell Addison what he was going to do and got a half-hearted agreement. The Lieutenant didn't seem to be much interested in the few hostiles at the rear of the train. His immediate concern seemed to be with the girl who was now serving in the double capacity of nurse and secretary.

Barry didn't like that idea any better than he had liked the odd conduct of Rossiter and Shingle. It was pretty evident that Shingle had just let his mask slip, showing resentment toward Barry. Rossiter had stepped in briskly to remind him. But why? What was their game? Certainly neither of them had any sort of decent feeling toward the man they were having to depend on. Barry reminded himself that he would have to check with Conway on the matter of the false death report. He felt certain that Jess had told him the word arrived in the east just a week after William Barry's death. Rossiter had since put the interval at six months.

They left armed teamsters on guard at the wagons, Samuels and Welland in charge. Samuels made no complaint about being left although Barry had expected something from him. Then he saw that the big Ohio trooper was sticking pretty close to Katie Hennessey. Somebody else was making a play for a nurse!

Corporal Wirtz went with the patrol, having become practically a member of the gang. They picked up Sawdust, got his report that no danger appeared in the west, and made a wide arc along the ridge to make sure that no elevation hid a lurking war party. The buffalo herd that had caused the alarm was still in sight, grazing a little over a mile from the river. Their evident peace was a good indication that no riders had come near them. Nor was there sign of movement anywhere else.

"Funny as hell," Sawdust grunted when they had almost completed the scouting trip. "This thing has got all the earmarks of a flankin' move, them varmints in the rear holdin' our attention while another gang sneaks up on us. But I'll swear there ain't no other red hide within miles. What the hell kin it mean?"

When they reached the spot where they could see down the river they saw that the Indians had halted when the wagons did, keeping about the same distance that they had maintained during the day. A pair of them sat their ponies on a bit of high ground, obviously keeping watch on the wagons, but the others had gone to the river and were letting their horses drink.

"Seems like they ain't much interested in us," Wirtz commented. "Kinda lazy and peaceful."

"They ain't actin' like Injuns at-all," Sawdust agreed.

Barry had been counting. He could see the entire dozen so he knew that none of them had undertaken any kind of sneak circling movement. "Let's see how they act if we ride at them," he suggested quietly. "Don't rush it and don't fire unless they show fight. Just keep riding at them and see what they do. Maybe we'll pick up a hint about their intentions."

"Or a bullet," Sawdust grunted. "We're with ye, Sarge."

CHAPTER 13

They swung into formation at Barry's order, riding five abreast down the trail with Barry at one end and Wirtz at the other. There was no sudden movement involved; they simply started riding straight at the Indians.

At once they could see a reaction to their performance. The warriors on lookout began to signal frantically. Two others who had been apparently gathering brush for a fire left off their work and climbed to the backs of their ponies. The others came up from the river in a hurry. There was a huddle that lasted a few minutes and then the Indians began to form a line of their own.

"Copyin' after us," Wirtz called to Barry. "Musta learned how to do comp'ny front."

"It won't last," Sawdust predicted. "They're jest gittin' into line so's all of them kin keep an eye peeled this way."

The ride continued at the same pace, the Indians waiting until the distance had been reduced by almost half. Then the warriors on the left of the line began to draw away from the others, climbing the ridge and drawing their line into wider spacing. By that time the crisp air made visibility so good that Barry began to make out details.

Sawdust called the shot before Barry could quite understand what he was seeing. "Damned few feathers on them bastards," the scout growled. "Seems like there ain't a real chief of any kind among 'em. Nobody's got any coups to brag about."

Barry hadn't remembered that adornment generally indicated past achievements of the warrior. Still he had been thinking along much the same line. It had seemed to him that the Indians were not very big. Somehow their movements had been a trifle odd. They had operated in a jerky sort of style as though nervously unsure of themselves.

"Half grown young warriors," he agreed.

"They musta rode on ahead of the big gang," Sawdust commented.

"But why?"

"Hard to tell. Ole Jim Bridger useta say that a white man can't understand what a Injun's thinkin' and a Injun don't know what a young Injun is thinkin' because the young Injun don't know what it is hisself 'til he does somethin' about it."

Barry chuckled. "That's kind of wordy for ole Jim Bridger," he laughed. "Generally he does better than that."

"Hell! Mebbe I didn't word it jest right."

"Next time you'll do better," Ladou consoled him.

Barry nodded in some satisfaction at the by-play. The men certainly weren't much worried about advancing on twice their number of hostiles.

The slow ride continued for another two hundred yards and then the Cheyennes began to fan out more rapidly, the flankers on their left climbing high on the ridge and beginning to close in so that the line became a long arc. Now the reds and yellows of barbaric adornment started to flash in the flattening rays of the sun and it occurred to Barry that here was a scene some competent artist should paint. He didn't waste much time on the thought. He was more concerned over searching for an explanation of the point he had discussed with Sawdust. Why was this band composed only of youngsters?

Others were thinking along the same lines. "Not a grown man among them," Strauss muttered loudly enough for the others to hear. "I think they are a little afraid of us."

"Don't count on it," Barry told him. "Sometimes it's the scared ones that do the most damage. Hold the pace but be ready to fall back in a hurry. We don't want to get cut off, even by children."

"And don't figger on 'em as childern," Sawdust put in. "Injun brats the age of these little bastards are the wust kind. They're out fer any kind o' hell that'll let 'em go back and brag like the reg'lar warriors. And they ain't got sense enough to take care o' their own hides doin' it. A lot of folks has got theirselves killed by young Injuns that didn't know no better than to attack when it looked foolish."

Now they could see that the left flank of the Cheyenne line was beginning to make the arc more pronounced. The strategy was clear enough. If the soldiers continued along the river trail they would have Indians on three sides of them with the river blocking the fourth side.

"This is far enough," Barry said in a quiet voice. "Pull up for a minute or two and let's see what they do."

When the soldiers halted the Indians did the same thing. The two forces studied each other from the medium distance, no one making any kind of move. "Let's go back," Barry ordered after a long pause. "They're making it pretty clear that they don't propose to attack but will circle us if we do. Swing around slowly and ride. Don't make it seem that we're running from them."

They followed orders, presently moving back upstream in the same five-abreast formation. The Indians promptly went back to the business of making camp. "Truce," Barry commented. "I wonder why?"

Before they reached the wagons Barry sent Ladou up the ridge as a sentry, the rest of them going on in to where the first decent meal in days had been prepared. Barry promptly called for a general conference to be held at the back of the wagon where Addison had his bed, almost everyone turning out with tin plates and food to make the whole thing seem like a social affair.

Barry told them what they had seen in the rear. "We can only guess what they're planning to do but with their small number it seems that sneak attacks can be expected. Tonight we double the guard but all pickets are to keep down and out of sight. These bucks will be just as eager to take a sentry scalp as any other kind."

"I still think it's a trap," Shingle growled. "It don't make a damned bit of difference that the devils behind us are young'uns. They're still keepin' us pinned down while some other crowd works around to cut us off. And it looks like they got a good chance to do it! We sure as hell stopped too early!"

"You know why!" Barry flared.

"I know what you claimed. I ain't so sure but what it's a damned rebel trick. Could be we even got Reb guerrillas movin' to cut us off."

In the moment of flat silence Sawdust drawled, "Ole Jim Bridger useta say that there wasn't nothin' like prejudices to cover up lack o' brains. A big mouth kin always hide a holler skull!"

Barry grinned. "I think you improved it a bit, Sawdust."

None of the others knew what he meant but most of them were still watching in perplexed silence. He took advan-

144

tage. "I know that a lot of you folks don't trust me even though it happens you're depending on me right now. Have it your own way, but don't start any more of that crazy scare talk. The army telegraph would have given plenty of warning if there had been any move by Confederate forces. Shingle can believe that we have hostiles ahead of us if he wants to. Maybe we do. But don't let any loud-mouthed idiot put extra fear into you with talk of troops!"

Shingle started to bluster but Rossiter was grabbing at his arm, trying to silence him. Again Barry seized the opportunity to make himself heard. "No point in arguing, Abe! I'm just as sick of your stupidity as you are of my interference. So shut up and let's get down to business.

"You've heard the obvious guess as to what these half-grown Indians are trying to do. I'll offer another. We know that at least two fair-sized war parties were not far east of us when we reached the river. We can be sure that they were met by the survivors of the morning fight. They know that we killed a lot of their braves so we expected them to give chase. That would mean they would send a strong party to harass us while the main force got into position for the big attack. They would not send children to do the holding job!"

There were nods as he made his point. Rossiter said loudly, "I think he's got it!"

"I think that these young warriors behind us are simply out to see if they can't count some coups on us, part of the usual thing a young brave has to do in making himself a real warrior. For some reason they're alone in the operation. For some reason the larger bands refused to turn back to chase us."

"What reason?" Conway asked.

"I can't even guess. Maybe it's the weather. Maybe they've got word of troops moving against their villages. Maybe the long expected reinforcements from the east are finally arriving."

"I think the man is right," Katie Hennessey broke in calmly. "I know that Colorado soldiers were going to attack Indian villages. We heard of the plans before we left Denver."

"It still could be rebels comin' up," Shingle growled.

"Oh, shut up!" It was Rossiter, his frown indicating that he was getting plenty annoyed at his wagon boss. Barry thought he knew why. Rossiter was planning something that would require temporary peace. He didn't want Shingle showing his hand.

"That's right, Herb," Conway broke in. "Keep his mouth out of this. Every time he opens up like that I think of the impression I got when this miserable war first started, that the loudest talking haters generally didn't know why they'd picked the side they did. Mostly they got drunk and committed themselves. Then they had to convince themselves they'd been right. So they talked big and loud."

Barry laughed. Featherstone wasn't the only philosopher in the crowd. It occurred to him that Conway hadn't come close to covering the subject. Others—like himself—had made their decisions just as foolishly without the excuse that they were drunk at the time. Maybe the only careful choosers had been the men who calculated coldly their chances of turning a profit out of the unhappy mess.

"Forget the side lines," he broke in, partly interrupting his own thoughts. "Right now all we ought to think about is the danger from sniping and scalping attempts. Sentries keep it in mind. Now let's get the details drawn and try for some sleep. It's going to be a long night."

To keep himself out of the spotlight he turned the guard assignment over to Wirtz, getting a brief nod from Addison as he turned toward the wagon. It was good to know that the Lieutenant approved of the way he had handled things but somehow it didn't matter very much.

He took plenty of time about eating his own delayed supper and while he was sitting silently by the fire Katie Hennessey came over to drop down beside him. "You handled that very nice," she told him with her faint accent showing.

"Thanks. How are your patients?"

She shook her head. "One will not live, I'm sure. The other will do well."

"Tell me what you heard about that militia expedition. Where are they planning to attack?"

She shrugged. "I heard only talk. We were not doing well at the time and I was more interested in getting away."

He knew a small curiosity about her but pushed it aside. "I'd like to know what we might expect from those Colorado boys. Didn't you hear any places mentioned?"

"I remember hearing of a place called Sand Creek. And the Arkansas. Does that help?"

"Not much, I'm afraid. It's possible that militia raids into that country would account for the Indians leaving but it's no certainty."

She turned to smile at him. "You figure out everything, don't you? I like that."

"Not everything," he replied. "I can't figure what a

woman like you would be doing on the eastbound trail with only a small party."

"Sometimes a woman like me has little choice. My husband decided."

"Unlucky for him."

"Maybe. Maybe he wasn't smart."

He waited to see what she was going to do in explaining it but she changed her tone just a little. "In this world a woman has to find a smart man if she hopes to get along. I made a mistake. The only good thing about marrying Hennessey was that it was a proper marriage. Next time I intend to be more careful."

Barry wondered what the unlamented Hennessey had done to put him out of the smart class but he didn't say anything. It was evident that the woman had something on her mind so he was willing to let her say it as she pleased.

"You're smart, Sergeant," she said after a pause. "I think you would be a good gamble—except for some things."

"Thanks. Meaning that I don't take off my overcoat when I go to bed?"

She laughed. "That was funny. For me, at least. Now that I know about you and Linda I assume it was not funny for you. When she came to us in the morning, I mean."

"Don't worry about it."

"I don't. For other women I have no pity. The competition is keen—and it will be keener with so many men being killed. I tell you frankly, Sergeant, that I had ideas about you. Now I'm not so sure that you would be a good man to choose. Perhaps your position is too vulnerable and your enemies too shrewd." She was rising as she spoke, her smile just a trifle awry as she turned away.

There had been no alarm when Wirtz wakened him for his turn as guard officer. They replaced their sentries as quietly as possible; then Wirtz and the first shift sought their blankets, glad to find a little warmth.

At midnight they relieved the pickets once more, still with no hint of trouble. Barry slept but little after that, his thoughts still a jumble of personal problems along with the responsibility of his temporary command. His brain kept asking innumerable questions but he managed to put them aside when he took over again at three o'clock. This time he made sure that he had his best men in key points. Strauss was at the rear along the trail. Wirtz remained on duty, taking a post on the ridge above Strauss. Ladou and Sawdust were higher on the ridge, opposite the wagon corral. Samuels with his lame leg covered the trail to the west. Each man was flanked at a little distance by one of the teamsters, Shingle and one man watching the river.

There was the slightest hint of gray in the eastern sky when the first alarm came. A single gunshot was followed by a yell of alarm and then a more distant shout. Barry drove hard up the ridge, certain that the yelling had been done by Indians. The guards had been cautioned not to do anything that would disclose their positions.

He found Ladou and Sawdust together, their story quickly told. A pair of raiders had tried to sneak across the ridge about halfway between the two men and Sawdust had taken a shot at them. He believed that he had wounded one of them but it had been too dark to be certain.

"Bastard sure sounded hurt," he said with a grim chuckle. "Either that or scareder'n hell."

They stopped talking to listen. Barry could make out a

distant rustle which Sawdust claimed was his victim being helped away. Ladou snorted disbelief. "Missed," he said shortly. "I hear bullet whiz."

"Ye're just spooked up 'cause ye was kinda in the line o' fire," Sawdust told him. "Likely asleep, at that."

They wrangled softly under the fading stars until Barry snapped an order for silence. "Still time for more trouble. Keep your eyes open."

He was starting back down the ridge when another shot cracked open the wall of morning silence. Again he galloped to investigate. He found Ben Samuels hunched down behind a rocky outcrop, staring toward the dark gulf which marked the river.

"Two-three of 'em tried to slip across," the trooper reported. "I heard 'em when they was on the other bank so I was ready. Soon as I seen somethin' in the water I cut loose. Don't reckon I hit nothin' but it seemed like a good idea to cut loose. Kinda discouraged 'em, I figure. They left."

The camp was now fully aroused so the wagoners began to make ready for the day's haul. Barry spoke to a couple of them as he rode through, sensing that some of the nervous tension had gone out of them again. Some of them even made jokes about scared guards firing at shadows. Barry was glad to have it that way. He went along with the humor, repeating his belief that the only danger now was from nuisance raids. He was beginning to think that it was the truth but the important thing was to get the men settled down so that they could handle their work and not let sudden scares upset them. Probably they would have to endure quite a bit more of this scare business.

CHAPTER 14

Barry went out with Sawdust just before the wagons were ready to roll, checking sign along the upper river and then cutting back along the line that had been under guard during the night. At the river they splashed across to the far side in their search, finding that Samuels had been right. Three Indians had come upstream on the far side and had attempted to cross after leaving their ponies some distance from the north bank. Then they had retreated in haste to their horses, evidently when Samuels fired.

On the ridge the sign was equally clear. Two Indians had crawled toward the wagons but had fled hurriedly, in this instance leaving spots of blood behind them. Sawdust had actually made good on his blind shot.

There was other sign to indicate that raiders had been moving in from several angles but it appeared that there had been a hasty withdrawal when the shooting started. These Indians had been pretty easy to discourage.

"More and more it looks like boy tricks," Barry said finally. "There's no point in what they're doing. No organization. Quick panic. I can't believe they're any part of a ruse. Just young hellions out for trouble."

"Which they found," Sawdust grunted. "I hope ye're right. Young'uns we kin handle, even with folks all full o' skeeriness."

When the train moved out there was no sign of the trailers. An hour later the dust began to show in the rear once more. By noon Wirtz had made a count of the pursuers. There were only nine of them now. With flat land all around it didn't seem possible that a flanking move was in prospect so the obvious guess was that the wounded Indian had been taken back by two of his comrades. There was still no indication of any larger party around.

Barry made his usual visit to Lieutenant Addison during the brief noon halt. Addison was dictating his report again and did not seem much interested in anything Barry had to tell him. Linda looked up from her notes just long enough to stare with what he guessed was studied annoyance. The only thing he could think of by way of rebuttal was to say, "See you later, Lieutenant. You'd better check Melinda Jessie's spelling. She never was very good at it." Then he went back to his duties.

Within the hour he knew that the continuing pressure was making itself felt. He wished that whatever Indian attack was coming would come and get it over with. A man could stand just so much of this constant tension, particularly when he had so many other things on his mind. Twice he found himself almost falling asleep in the saddle, each time riding to another part of the train to shake off the dullness. None of it seemed to help.

Then he saw Sawdust signaling from his advance position. Barry came alert in an instant, shouting a warning to the teamsters as he spurred toward the lanky scout. The train was to continue unless a gunshot warned them to corral.

"Dust," Sawdust told him briefly. "Still outa sight behind them low ridges."

Without a further exchange of words they swung to send their horses up a sandy slope that would give them a better look at the road ahead. There they waited until the dust cloud came up from behind the nearer ridge.

"Two men, looks like," Sawdust muttered. "I can't see no more'n that."

"Only two," Barry agreed. "And they're not Indians. Let's go."

It didn't take long to discover that the approaching pair were somewhat elderly farmers, both heavily armed and looking dangerous enough in spite of their garb. The smaller one, wearing patched bib overalls and knee boots, seemed to be the spokesman for the pair. He talked in a jerky fashion, the wagging of a pointed white beard adding to the impression that his words were coming out in some mechanical fashion.

"Glad to see . . . blue uniforms," he told them. "Didn't figure as . . . how ye'd ever git through. Been a lot o' war parties . . . all around lately. Name's Ezekiel Schelter. This here's Parker." He dismissed his companion as not really worthy of much attention. Parker was almost twice as big as Schelter but his round face seemed curiously blank and he said nothing when his name was mentioned.

"You knew we were looking for the lost wagons?" Barry asked.

"Sure. Got word . . . f'm Fort Laramie. Wanted us to . . . send out help . . . but we don't have nobody . . . 'cept us old coots, that is."

It took a little while for him to sputter out the details but when he was finished Barry felt that he knew a lot of answers. The more active militiamen from the area north of Denver had been called down toward the capital a month earlier, leaving the area around old Fort Lupton to be guarded by old men and boys. With strong parties of hostiles in the neighborhood they had been in no position to do anything about lost wagons. Today was the first that any scouting party had moved so far east. Schelter and Parker had volunteered to find out whether the Indians had actually gone away as somewhat more timid scouting parties had reported.

"I reckon Colonel Chivington's hit . . . them Cheyenne towns," Schelter boasted, the whiskers brushing hard at the bib of his overalls. "The red devils musta . . . skeedaddled fer their villages . . . when they heard tell what . . . was happenin' back there."

"Let's get this straight," Barry broke in, watching over his shoulder as the wagons came on, their drivers aware that white men had been met. "Are you telling me that the Indians have left this part of the country because Colorado troops have made a campaign against the Indian villages?"

"That's about the size of it."

"What villages?"

"Dunno exactly. Regiment went southeast outa Denver mebbe a week ago. They wasn't tellin' nobody where they went." For the first time he got it out all in one breath.

Barry nodded, glancing around at Sawdust. "I think we guessed right. Those big bands had heard about the attacks on their villages. When the survivors of that first fight met them they couldn't find anybody willing to come back for another try. Only a pack of ornery young whelps decided to have a try at picking up some scalps."

"Sounds like it." He turned to ask Schelter a question. "Ye sure them milishy rode out a week ago?"

The little man shrugged. "Coulda been a mite more. Our boys went to join 'em a good fortnight ago. Why?"

Sawdust shrugged his lank shoulders. "Fer us I reckon it don't make much difference 'ceptin' that now we ain't got no Injuns on our tails but a few nits and lice. Fer other folks this could stir up a lot more hell than they been havin'."

"How do you figure?" Barry demanded.

"Easy. The villages what got hit musta been the same ones what had most o' their warriors out here raisin' hell. The Colorado boys musta caught nobody home but squaws and kids."

"Jest like what the Injuns done to us," Schelter snapped.

"Sure—but that ain't the point. The warriors will be mad as hell. Instead o' holin' up fer the winter and givin' us a breathin' spell, mebbe lettin' us git some extry men out here, they'll go hawg-wild!"

"Suits us," Schelter told him. "Injuns never was wuth a damn at winter fightin'. We'll beat the tar out of 'em if they try it."

Barry felt curiously let down. His first sight of the armed settlers had given him a feeling that he was through with his troubles. The wagons were out of danger and his responsibility was over. It wasn't a matter of thought because he knew better. It was simply a feeling. Now he knew that he could expect more complications. With a winter campaign probable he would have less hope than before of getting a chance to go east.

"How far to the nearest settlement?" he asked, forcing his thoughts away from personal troubles. "Where's the telegraph line?"

"Mebbe twenty miles to our place," Schelter told him. "We cut away across the bend of the Platte. Nearest reg'lar telegraph is at old Fort Lupton—or what's left of it. Relay station a mite closer."

"And no hostiles between here and the settlement?"

"We ain't seen none. And no sign."

"Are you in any rush to get home?"

"Not partickler. Couldn't make it . . . not tonight, nohow."

"Then how about riding along with our wagons for a while? You'll make folks feel a bit better to hear what you can tell them. They've had a rough time."

"Sure. Me'n Parker . . . We ain't in no hurry."

Barry left then, he and Sawdust riding to pass the word to the flankers. No more was said about Featherstone's grim predictions. For the moment it was better to keep everybody happy that the worst was over.

The balance of the day was quiet, even the chill easing a little so that physical comfort was added to emotional relief. The little band of brash young Indians still hung on the rear, never getting closer but never leaving. Barry and his men maintained vigilance. In dealing with such fellows the foolish attack might be the one most to be expected.

The train halted at a creek, having left the river in order to cut more directly toward Denver. There was decent water and the camp became almost lively. The strain was gone. Meeting a pair of armed farmers had done more for morale than the added safety warranted. Lieutenant Addison sat up to get his supper and one of the wounded teamsters climbed out of his wagon to take a few steps around the camp. Mrs. Hennessey's report that her other patient probably would not live through the night drew scant attention. One personal tragedy could not destroy the general air of satisfaction. Only Rossiter and Shingle did not seem to share the ease. They talked together most of the time, taking no part in any of the conversations around the fires.

"You should keep an eye on those men," Katie Hennessey told Barry when she had occasion to pass him. "I overheard just enough to make me understand that they are concerned about you."

"Thanks. I think you're right and I'll be watching."

"I told you that you were smart. Now I wonder if you are smart enough to know how they think?"

Barry grinned. "I'll guess. They've been playing nice to me because they needed me. Now I'm not so important to them so they'll start trying a new angle."

She nodded. "You're smart," she agreed. "I can regret that other things don't work out so well."

He was left to guess at what she meant because she hurried on about her own affairs while he set at the chore of getting sentinels organized for the night. It made no difference that no real war party was nearby. While those young hellions were on the flanks anything could happen. A man could die just as dead in a nuisance raid as in a big battle.

Again he turned the early evening over to Wirtz, finding a spot beneath Addison's wagon where he might get some sleep before turning out for his turn as guard officer. He felt sore, utterly weary, when Sawdust shook him out of a sound sleep but he realized that he was experiencing reaction to the long days and nights of pressure. What he needed was about twelve hours of uninterrupted rest. At the moment it seemed like a minor tragedy that he would probably have to wait several more days before he could get it.

Oddly enough he thought about Katie Hennessey. She

had sounded pretty serious with her warning even though there had been that definite hint of coquetry in it. Did she really know something? He had a feeling that she might. The woman was pretty sharp with her observation and she managed to get around quite a lot. He decided that he ought to ask Samuels about her. The Ohioan had been giving her plenty of attention.

Then he remembered that Sawdust was trying to shake him into wakefulness, obviously to tell him that it was time for him to take over from Corporal Wirtz.

"Midnight already?" he muttered drowsily.

Sawdust laughed. "Goin' to be daylight in a bit more'n an hour. We kinda figgered ye could use the sleep."

Barry came up in a hurry. "I didn't . . . What did . . . ?"

"Don't sputter, Sarge. Ye needed the rest and anyhow I got orders from the lootenint. He claimed he was feelin' real peert and didn't need to sleep nohow. So he's been orderin' out the watches and lettin' you sleep."

"But he didn't . . ."

"Nope. He's been in the wagon on the blankets like Miss Conway insisted. But he could send out orders. Wirtz and me passed 'em along. Everything's been plenty quiet."

Barry had his wits about him by that time. "Relief routed out yet?"

"Sure. They're finishin' their coffee. Better go tell the lootenint ye're up. By that time it'll be a good idea to fill in the guard line without relievin' anybody. Them hellions have got to hit this mornin' or not at all."

"Be with you in a minute." He hurried out from under the wagon and spoke into the dark interior. "Thanks, Lieutenant. I needed the sleep. Maybe more than I realized."

"I know you did." The tone was formal but there was a shade of warmth in it. "Sorry I couldn't relieve you sooner. Understand that you're still in active command of the train."

There was time for Barry to have the satisfaction of feeling that he had really changed Addison's mind about himself. Then Linda's voice came from somewhere in the interior darkness. "Do you think we'll finally be out of danger today, Tom?"

Two days earlier he would have liked to hear that casualness in her tone. Now he would almost have preferred to have her continuing to snap at him. She was being almost friendly, as was Addison. Maybe they had ceased to resent him because they had found something else to keep them happy.

"We'll hope so," he said gruffly. "This morning tells the story. We've got to be ready if those young hellions try to get in a few spite licks."

He started to turn away but Addison spoke quickly. "What's your opinion about this Colorado expedition, Sergeant? Featherstone hinted that he feared that it would stir up worse troubles."

"I get most of my opinions from Private Featherstone, sir," Barry told him with just a shade of stiffness. "Generally he's right."

When there was no reply he moved away to the fire and coffee. The extra guard detail was waiting, teamsters and soldiers now on good terms with each other. Still they were showing a shade of the old tension, all of them well aware that the morning might bring a last surge of trouble. It would be the last practical chance for the hostiles to try anything.

Practically everyone in the wagon outfit was awake, whether they were to go on guard duty or not. Abe Shingle stood a little to one side, a rifle in the crook of his arm. Rossiter was just coming from his wagon. Conway was with the men at the fire. Wirtz came in from the up-river end of the camp, ready to assist with placing the new men.

"Take care of it, Corporal," Barry told him. "You've been running things fine so far; no reason for me to break in now. I'll just move along from one place to another as dawn begins to show."

He turned for a word with the wagon boss while Wirtz took over the assignment of posts. "You've got men covering the river, Shingle?" he asked.

The wagon boss growled assurance without even looking up. Today he didn't seem to think it worth while to go on with the pretense of good humor. Maybe he knew that he hadn't done too well with the pose or perhaps it was as Katie Hennessey had called it; he didn't need to care now that he wasn't depending on Barry to protect his wagons from any major danger. Barry wanted to tell him that he could soon become normally offensive but he didn't think it was a good idea to stir up any unnecessary trouble.

He began to make a circuit of the guard positions, paying special attention to the posts along the ridge. That was where he thought an attack might develop, the Indians using the rougher ground to cover their approach. It was chilly up there where an early morning breeze was getting a sweep at the higher ground but the alert sentries did not seem to mind. They were more interested in the quietness of the pre-dawn darkness. Even the coyotes weren't sounding off very much.

It took better than a half hour to cover the whole line but there was still no real sign of dawn when he began to work back over the ridge once more. He was walking softly, keeping a little below the ridge summit except as he moved in to speak in whispers with the men on watch. He had reached the upstream end of the line when he knew that a dark figure was just below him, between himself and the wagon trail.

He pulled up short, waiting and straining his ears for some sound of movement that would tell him that his eyes had not deceived him. Then he heard something that was little more than the whisper of fabric rubbing against itself. The unknown was being extremely cautious, almost furtive in his movements, and Barry dropped into a crouch, pulling his revolver as he did so.

For a moment or two he froze in that position but then realized that he must be silhouetted against the sky. He had not expected to deal with an enemy at that angle so he was caught foul. The whisper of fabric came again, this time with the soft scrape of a boot heel on loose gravel. Barry took a quick look and made his move, aware that the gray of dawn would make his present position worse. He still did not know what to expect from the stealthy figure on the slope below him but it seemed like a good idea to jump for the shadow of some nearby mesquite.

The move must have been exactly what the stalker needed. There was a yellow flare of muzzle blast and with it a lance of pain across the back of Barry's shoulder. He was dimly conscious of the gunshot noise and of a quick realization that his bent-over position had let the slug go partly over his shoulder and back. Then he was falling forward, trying to sight for a return shot even as he went down.

Something brought sudden pain to the side of his face and he fought to steady himself, knowing that he was sliding headlong down the slope. His assailant fired again and this time Barry saw the shadow behind the spurt of orange flame. He dug toes into the gravel and slowed his slide, aiming at the same time. He was aware of firing two quick shots with the revolver but then the dizziness caught him and he knew that he was sliding again.

CHAPTER 15

The blackness never quite closed down on him. He felt sick, a little weak, almost too tired to care about anything. Then he heard running feet as someone came laboring up the slope, calling, "Anybody hurt? Who fired that shot?"

It was Jess Conway's voice and Barry managed to answer. "Up here, Jess," he hailed, his voice sounding strange in his own ears. "I'm hit—but not bad. Somebody took a shot at me from inside the picket line. Pass the word."

Conway was bawling the alarm and orders as he panted to a halt, unable to get breath for questions after the double effort. Barry found his head clearing so he sat up, feeling gingerly at his shoulder. There was blood but he could use the arm. It didn't even hurt very much but he guessed that shock might be deadening the pain.

"Tell them to look sharp for the Cheyennes near the wagons," he told Conway. "That shot came from farther down the ridge. Toward the corral."

More help arrived promptly and in the fading gloom he saw that Katie Hennessey had accompanied one of the drivers. She took charge with some briskness, seeing to it that Conway and the teamster hurried the wounded man down the slope. "Got to get at the wound," she said. "He's losing blood."

The whole camp was in an uproar by that time but there was no sign of an Indian. In the midst of the noise Lieutenant Addison's voice shouted, "Bring him over here. Corporal Wirtz! Featherstone! Split the guard line between you and take command out there!"

The words seemed to come through a haze to Barry but he found himself hoping that the two soldiers would know what Addison meant. If they didn't they'd figure out something.

Katie Hennessey turned as they reached the level ground and started through the wagon line. "Are you all right, Sergeant?"

He forced a reply. "Sure. Just a scratch. Seems like I ducked just in time so the bullet almost missed me."

"You should have ducked harder," Conway panted in his ear. "There's a hell of a lot of blood runnin' down your back."

Linda came out to give them a hand, waving away the men who had brought him in. "Take care of your duties. Katie and I can take over from here. Just put him there on those blankets."

"Careful," Barry called after the two men. "Don't let any wild shooting get started. In a few minutes it'll be light enough to know what's what." The effort silenced him for some little time after that.

For the next ten minutes or so there was a brisk stir of activity at the rear of the wagon where Addison now waited impatiently. The women were still working by lantern light although the yellow gleam had become useless as the dawn faded out the feebler effort. Barry knew that they had stripped him of his upper garments and that he was cold. Beyond that he was not too sure about anything, the combination of shock and continued fatigue making him a little vague about the whole affair.

Finally he began to understand what the women were saying. He knew that Linda was directing the job, doing most of the actual work while Katie Hennessey acted as helper. Evidently the wound was in the muscles at the base of the neck rather than in the shoulder proper. It had bled freely but was still only a flesh wound.

"You're going to have precious little use for that right arm during the next two weeks or so," Linda told him when she saw that he was fully conscious once more. "I think there's considerable injury to the right shoulder and neck muscles. Try not to turn your head or raise your right arm."

"Yes, Doctor," he agreed meekly. He wondered where she had picked up her easy assurance on medical matters. Then he remembered that he knew nothing of what she had been doing in the past three years. The Sanitary Commission had been mighty active in Tennessee during that time. It seemed likely that Linda had seen something of war.

They finished the intricate job of bandaging, Linda still calling the play and the blonde woman murmuring occasional appreciation of the way it was all being done. Finally she told Linda, "I never saw that kind of bandaging done before. It's real clever."

"The only way to make it stay in place for such a wound." The dark-haired girl stood up, meeting Barry's eyes then for just a moment. "First time I ever put one on a rebel though."

Addison's voice came in pretended sharpness from the wagon. "You're talking about a soldier of my command, Miss! Please use a little care."

Surprisingly, Linda winked. Then she turned and went out of Barry's range of vision. Immediately Katie Hennessey knelt beside him, her voice a cautious whisper. "Did you know it wasn't any Indian who shot you, Sergeant?"

Barry looked up with something of an effort. The shock was wearing off and the pain was beginning to tear at him. He didn't want to think. "I saw a shadow," he muttered. "Couldn't tell much."

"I think it was Abe Shingle. He slipped out of camp when he thought no one was watching him. And he carried his rifle."

The cobwebs seemed to part slightly. "Shingle!" Barry exclaimed. "I should have known!"

"As you said earlier. When he no longer needed you to take care of the train he would try to do something."

"At Rossiter's orders, damn it!" He was trying to keep the fog from coming in on his brain again. It was easy to remember how Rossiter and Shingle had tried to play friendly while they needed his help against hostile Indians. Rossiter's promise to be honest with him had been part of the act. Now . . .

A yell from just beyond the wagon circle interrupted the hazy circle of thoughts. He listened long enough to know what had happened. Somebody had finally stumbled on Shingle's body. The man was dead. Barry found that his only reaction was a somewhat smug satisfaction. Not bad shooting to hit a man in the dark under such circumstances. Too bad it hadn't been Rossiter. Then the fog closed in again and he stopped thinking about anything.

When he opened his eyes full daylight had arrived. The wagons were ready but no one had ordered a move. Guards and teamsters alike stood around finishing their breakfasts, only a couple of sentries having been left out. Obviously there had been no Indian attack of any kind.

Suddenly he remembered his own condition and the circumstances behind it. He wondered what had been done about the finding of Shingle's body but for the moment there was no one near him to answer any questions. Then Linda Conway hurried over with a cup of coffee, bracing his head as she held it for him. "There's a lot of hard talk about what happened, Tom," she said in a quiet voice. "You can imagine how it goes. Some think it was all a horrible mistake. Some blame you and some believe that Shingle tried to murder you."

"What's your opinion?"

"Does it matter?"

"Of course. You have believed a lot of hard things about me in the past. I'm hoping this will be different."

"I agree with my father. He has come right out and accused Rossiter of plotting your murder."

There was no time for more talk. A couple of teamsters and Sawdust came over to carry Barry to the same wagon Addison was occupying. Linda saw to it that they lifted him in such a manner as to avoid putting any strain on the injured neck muscles. Still the move brought on the dizziness once more and by the time he was settled on a blanket he knew only that the girl was working at the bandages, probably because the bleeding had started again.

When he got his wits about him next he saw that Sawdust was riding directly behind the wagon. He started to call out but Linda put her fingers gently against his lips.

"Quiet," she warned. "We're an hour on the trail. Don't try to talk. Just listen."

"What about the Indians?" he asked as soon as she removed her hand.

"Forget them," Addison's voice replied. "Our scouts report that the Indians stopped following us early last evening. The trail is clear. They simply gave up."

Sawdust nodded from his position behind the wagon. "Seems like Abe had it figgered wrong if'n he was aimin' to gun ye down and blame it on the Cheyennes. We're keepin' an eye on that fat polecat so don't fret about what he'll try to do."

"Thanks," Barry murmured. He didn't feel up to talking. It was hard enough to think. All that came clear in his mind was that he still had no hold on Herbert Rossiter. There would be no way of proving that he even knew about Shingle's plan to kill the man who stood in his way.

Sawdust rode away then and presently Linda began to talk, explaining that she had been going over the facts with her father. Conway was now convinced that he had teamed up with a thief—and worse. He wanted Barry to know as much as possible about the business end of things, hopeful that between them they might find a way to stop Rossiter's schemes.

The Rossiter-Conway deal was an equal partnership. Conway's share of the investment had been close to fifty thousand dollars. Rossiter's share had been roughly the same, both figures complicated by the problem of putting true values on property while wartime inflation drove markets crazy. Their plan had been to get one train into the west before the winter, thus allowing the new company to set up a headquarters somewhere in the Denver area but with other offices farther west. Rossiter had gone as far as Salt Lake City in preparing that part of it. With offices thus set up they would be ready to move with other goods in the spring—or whenever the war should end.

"Sounds like you've got something to fight for," Addison commented. "There must be plenty of valuable property still in the east. This train can't represent much of the total assets. Do you have any idea what part of the Rossiter share is actually yours?"

Linda answered the question. "My father says that Rossiter implied that his deal with William Barry was also a fifty-fifty one."

"A claim he didn't plan to let me make," Barry growled.

"Don't worry about the business," Linda told him. "Father knows how things stand. This was your idea in the first place and he's not going to see you cheated out of your proper share."

Barry didn't reply. He had confidence in Jess Conway but there were limits to what Conway could do. The man might control his half of the company but he didn't have much to say about the other half.

The wagons halted a little longer at noon than they had been doing. Partly that was because they no longer felt the pressure to hurry toward safety. The other reason was that the teamster Katie Hennessey had been nursing had finally died. They buried him beside the trail. No one had known him very well so there were no formalities. Just another trailside grave had been added to the already large number.

Barry slept most of the day, waking to find that the wagons were going to camp just outside a grubby sort of settlement. Some of the houses were a sod and frame combination like most of the dwellings along the Platte but others were real log cabins. With the mountains now showing their early snow crests not far to the west nobody needed to be told that the treeless plains were behind. Now they could swing south and aim for those profitable Denver markets.

Lieutenant Addison declared himself able to move around with an improvised crutch and left the wagon as soon as he learned that they were quite close to the army's telegraph relay station. "Time I did something like duty," he told Barry. "I'll try to find out whatever I can from Captain Pritchard as soon as I take care of my regular report."

Barry was not particularly interested in anything Pritchard might have discovered. The facts were clear enough now. What he needed was a chance to do something about it. Probably he could have taken care of his own interests here in the west—with Jess Conway's help—but those legal tangles back east were another matter entirely. Rossiter and his grafting friends would have covered their tracks carefully and it would take somebody with plenty of influence and prestige to even undertake an investigation.

The hopelessness of it left him with a bitterness that he

had not felt even in his days at Rock Island prison. Now he knew the facts. He understood his enemy and knew what the enemy had done. But he couldn't do a thing about it. No soldier could hope for leave to travel east just now. And no Galvanized Yankee could expect to turn up at a Federal supply depot and make charges against a man who had enough influence to have wires sent on his behalf to places like Fort Laramie.

While he was thinking about the hopelessness of it there was an interruption. Conway and Rossiter appeared at the open back of the wagon, Conway asking quietly, "Got yourself together enough to talk, Tom?"

Barry tried to see the fat man's face in the dim light. "If talk will do any good," he replied.

"We'll talk whether you like it or not!" Rossiter snapped. "I've been hearing some damned ugly talk today. Some of your precious friends are claiming that I sent Shingle to kill you."

"Didn't you? It's a cinch he didn't take me for an Indian!"

"And you didn't take him for one! You're the murderer, not Shingle!"

"Plenty of men heard the shots," Barry told him. "Men who can tell the difference between the sound of a rifle and a pistol. No question about who fired first. No question about which one of us was where he wasn't supposed to be."

"That's neither here nor there. I'm warning you that if you permit libelous statements to be made against me I'll have you in court the minute we reach civilization!"

Conway broke in anxiously. "Let's not get hasty, either of

170

you. Herb, you promised to settle fairly with Tom, didn't you?"

"Fairly? I wonder what you think that means? His father put precious little into our deal. I'm the one who saved him what he had. I'm the one who made the company what it was. Do you expect me to hand out charity to a rebel who lets his disreputable companions blackguard me?"

"Then your promise means nothing?" Barry asked, keeping his voice low.

"I made no binding promise. You can't hold me to a thing!"

"So now we understand each other. Now I'll make you a promise and I'll consider it binding. I'm going to raise every bit of stink I can about you. I'll bet that an investigation will show that it was my father who put up most of the capital for your partnership. I wouldn't be surprised to learn that all you put in was your political influence in getting his just claims paid and perhaps in landing contracts after the company was started."

"Big talk!" Rossiter jeered. "Wild guesses. You can't prove a word of it."

"And I can't prove that you sent Shingle out to kill me but I'm sure you did. I think you also bribed somebody to fake that casualty report so you could claim the partnership property. Nothing else accounts for the way you got worried when you found that you had to travel in the Fort Laramie area. You were worried when you found that I was guarding your stagecoach but you were more than worried when it turned out that I might be sent south where I'd run across the Conways. You tried hard to keep me off the patrol with your crazy talk about rebel plots."

"Prove it!" the fat man snarled.

Barry ignored the interruption. "So you had to play for time. That was the reason you made that break the other morning and aroused the Indians. You hoped that you'd get me killed. Three other men died because of your effort but you didn't get rid of me. After that you had to wait some more because you needed me. Finally you sent Shingle to do the job."

"I don't have to listen to such nonsense!" Rossiter shouted. "Conway, you'd better warn this young fool to mind his tongue."

"He sounds mighty convincing to me," Conway retorted. "Maybe he could convince other people."

"I'll have the pair of you in court! I'll . . ."

"Wait a bit!" a nasal voice broke in. "Seems like a man oughta figger a bit. Ain't no courts around here. Could be ye'll never git to one."

"Never mind, Sawdust," Barry said quietly. "Don't make threats. Just keep an eye on him."

"I'll do that, Sarge. Come along, ye fat sonofabitch! Ye're disturbin' a wounded man."

Barry could not be certain but the grunting and cursing let him guess that Sawdust was escorting his charge around the wagon in a distinctly forceful manner.

"Chips are down," Conway growled. "I wonder what we ought to do next?"

CHAPTER 16

They had come to no decent conclusion when Lieutenant Addison came back to the wagon, helped from the saddle and onto his blankets by Strauss and Ladou. In spite of his own preoccupation Barry had to notice the good humor with which both men handled him and the grateful friendliness in Addison's voice. At least one good development had come out of this job.

Addison seemed exhausted after his long session with the army telegraph operator. He simply said, "I'm weak as a cat," and then he stretched out in silence for several minutes as though trying to get his strength back.

Then he spoke again. "Not much for you, Barry. Captain Pritchard can't get many personal messages through. Too much on the wire. All he knows is that they've found evidence that your name was added to a casualty list after it was originally made up."

"Good. That's a starter. If I can prove that maybe I can prove some other things. Did we get orders?"

Addison chuckled. "Several lots. The first ones I protested on the grounds that you and I are badly wounded and will not be able to travel for some weeks." His chuckle came again as he said, "I begin to see how you fellows have handled things out here. A man can't be too finicky about facts. Anyway, you and I are to remain with the wagons—as our ambulances—until we reach Denver. Then we get further orders after seeing a certain surgeon at that point. I hoped you might make something of that much delay."

"Thanks for trying, Lieutenant. It sounds like you've been having some of the outcast rub off on you. And what about them? My men, I mean?"

"They're to march north immediately. The post has not received any reinforcements but the general idea is that the

Indian raids have ended for this year. Apparently this Colorado militia strike was a big one. They've hit the Indians hard and headquarters thinks the blow will drive the remaining hostiles into their winter villages."

"You mean Chivington really defeated a big bunch of warriors?"

"That's the way the talk runs. He's claiming a major victory. Anyway, our headquarters has ordered resumption of mail service along all lines. Captain Pritchard wants as many men for guard details as he can get. I'm to send the men north with Corporal Wirtz in command. The adjutant's a bit anxious that they get up through the badlands before more snow can come along."

There was quite a bit more, Addison getting it out gradually between rest periods. The news from the east was much the same as it had been. Sherman was within striking distance of Savannah, Confederate resistance having almost completely collapsed in front of him. Grant still had Richmond partly bottled up and Lee's army was short of horses, provisions, and men. Sheridan had made a shambles of the Shenandoah valley, destroying the stores which Lee needed so badly. Still there was no indication that anyone in the Confederate government was talking surrender.

For Barry that was bad. His only chance of making his way east in an effort to straighten out his business affairs was for the war to end. While it continued he was still in an awkward position.

That night he learned that his position was no more comfortable than it had been with the wagoners. People from the settlement drifted out to the wagon camp, partly out of curiosity and partly because they wanted to talk about the big news. Their militia had struck a hard blow at the Cheyennes. The evil machinations of Confederate agents had been squelched by the Chivington raid. They were triumphant but no less bitter about the white men they blamed for the Indian outrages. Barry was just as well pleased that none of them came to visit him.

Addison issued marching orders to the men who were to head north, careful to remind Wirtz that he would do well to depend on Featherstone. The brawny corporal nodded easily. He had come to think of himself as a part of the somewhat disreputable little fraternity. He had struck up a friendship with Samuels and was on joking terms with Ladou.

"I'll be boss, Lieutenant," he said soberly. "But I'm figgerin' to have Sawdust tell when to do the bossin'. Right sir?"

"That'll do. I've already reported everything by wire. The post commander knows what a good job all of you have done. Just get back without running into any trouble and I'll be happy."

"One thing, Lieutenant. Is it all right with you if we could git ourselves outfitted with them six-shooters like the Sarge's men have got? They sure beat sabers in a tight fight."

"You mean you know where you can buy what you want? They're not army issue, you know."

"We got a deal in mind, sir," Wirtz told him. "I reckon we could swing it. Only Welland and me needs 'em."

Addison seemed about to offer some kind of protest but then he shut his mouth and simply nodded. When Wirtz and the others hurried away he turned toward Barry in the darkness and muttered, "I'll bet money they're planning to steal the weapons."

"No bet," Barry told him. "I'm afraid the corporal has been exposed to bad influences. It's a shame my men haven't been able to keep him away from the wrong kind of people."

Addison laughed. Then he said in a strange voice, "I wonder why I think that's funny? I'd have been a bit outraged by the whole idea not so long ago . . . not to mention that matter of exaggerating certain matters on the telegraph."

Linda Conway came along with supper for both men, hearing their laughter and joining in with some banter of her own. "I think I'm wasting my time giving you so much service. Both of you sound quite able to get up and take care of yourselves without nursing."

"And both of us are smart enough to know a good thing when we see it," Addison retorted. "Fort Laramie was never like this!"

"I'm sorry I have to spoil this fine display of cheerfulness," she said in an altered tone. "But the fact is that Mrs. Hennessey has been spending the past two hours with Rossiter, except for the short time when he was over here at this wagon."

"Any idea what's up?" Barry asked quickly.

"I couldn't really snoop," the girl said with some show of heat. "After all, I'm not the one who's likely to be jealous of her."

Barry grimaced in the darkness. "Forget the petty digs, Linda. You know how much . . . but we won't talk about that now. How is she acting? It could be that she's decided to throw in with him."

"But why? Scarcely anyone in the train believes anything except that he sent Abe Shingle to shoot you."

"And got away with it. Katie figures things out. She wants a man who's going to succeed. I'd say that she has decided to put her money on Rossiter."

"But . . ."

"The odds are with her," Barry said shortly. "Maybe she's a smart gambler."

Sawdust and Ladou came to the wagon then, on the surface acting as messengers for Wirtz and asking permission to leave before dawn next morning so as to get through the really bad country during the daylight hours. Barry felt pretty certain that the direct route north had no seriously bad country along it but he didn't say so. He was touched that the men had found an excuse to say their good-byes so he joked with them a while and then shook hands with both of them. Sawdust closed it out with, "We'll be lookin' fer ye soon, Sarge. And fer the lootenint too."

When they were gone into the darkness Addison murmured, "I think I've been given an accolade or something. That rascal sounded almost sincere."

"He was," Barry told him. "Maybe it's a good thing they're leaving. In another few days you might have found yourself adopted into the most unmilitary squad on the frontier."

"I could do worse," Addison retorted.

Barry fell asleep quickly, his own troubles pushed aside by his amusement at the new Addison. It seemed only moments later that he was awakened as Wirtz and the detail came to report their departure. Addison had no extra orders for them so there were only quick "so longs" and then the men faded into the pre-dawn darkness. Barry found himself awake enough to wonder. He had not heard either Sawdust or Ladou and it did not seem that there had been quite enough bulk of shadows. He wondered—but then he fell asleep again.

The usual morning chores were in progress when he opened his eyes again. He moved his head gingerly, knowing that such movements during the night had brought him into pained wakefulness. The neck wound was not serious but it was going to be painful enough to be mighty awkward. He let himself relax again, listening to the small buzz of activity in the camp. There was no rush this morning, no excitement. The wagon people were taking their own good time about getting started.

Minutes later he sensed a difference in the hum of voices. At first he couldn't guess what it meant but then he decided that a search of some sort was being made. Conway confirmed the guess quickly as he came to the wagon to ask, "Any idea why Rossiter's missing?"

"No. Are you sure he's missing?"

"Sure. He's not in his wagon. I got a man checking the horses right now. Maybe he's decided to beat us into Denver and make some kind of a deal on his own hook."

Barry ignored the tug of pain as he rolled to one side and began to slide out over the back of the wagon. "Shove my boots on for me, will you, Jess. I'm getting up."

He was on the ground, trying to shake off a trace of dizziness, when he asked, "Anybody talk to Mrs. Hennessey yet? She was with him last night and maybe she'll know what he's up to."

"I didn't see her around."

A teamster met them before they had gone fifty feet, reporting that no horses seemed to be missing except the army mounts which the troops had taken with them. Conway thanked the man and headed straight for Rossiter's wagon. "Let's see what he took with him. All I heard was that he wasn't in his wagon."

Several of the men joined them as they moved. Barry saw that Linda had come out to watch from a little distance while her mother pretended to be busy starting breakfast. Katie Hennessey was nowhere to be seen.

It was Conway who climbed into the wagon, his first expression one of quick surprise. "What the hell! Looks like his clothes are right where he took 'em off last night! Nothin' missing but him!"

"What about Shingle's stuff?" Barry asked, making himself stay on one side where there would be no temptation to strain his neck looking. "This was Shingle's sleeping quarters to begin with. Maybe Rossiter used Shingle's gear."

Another exclamation came from the wagon and Conway moved into the interior. Then he exclaimed, "One of you men! Give me a hand here."

By that time everyone except Barry was trying to see into the wagon. There was a mutter of curiosity as a teamster crawled in out of sight. Then a woman's voice broke the heavier tone of the audience. Barry knew that he was hearing Katie Hennessey. He also heard one of the outside watchers grunt, "Nekkid as an aig under that blanket! What the hell went on around here?"

"Where are my clothes?" Mrs. Hennessey was demanding angrily. "Who did this to me?"

Conway growled, "We were hopin' you could tell us. Where's Rossiter?"

"I don't know." There was a pause before she said, "That's mine. Hand it over here and get out. All I know is that I went to sleep in here. Some time during the night I heard a noise. Before I could do any more than ask a question somebody held me down and put that rag around my mouth. After that I was rolled up in this blanket and tied. I couldn't move. I could hardly breathe!"

"What about Rossiter? Was he in here with you?"

"Of course! And I don't know what happened to him. Now get out and let me get into some clothing."

Conway came out with a crooked grin showing. "She was tied up like a mummy," he told Barry. "But without a stitch on her underneath the blanket. Rossiter's clothes are all in there, so far as I could tell."

Barry turned to look at the grinning faces around him. "Any of you men good at tracking? Scout around a bit and see if you can find traces of anybody leaving the wagon camp."

There was a reluctant scattering. Barry didn't know whether the men were more interested in the fact that Katie Hennessey had shared Rossiter's sleeping quarters or that she had been wearing nothing under the blanket. He wasn't so sure just which point was more interesting.

While the search was being pressed Schelter and Parker came out from the settlement to say goodbye to the wagoners. They promptly took over the tracking job and presently found a trail which led off to the south. Two horses had walked away from the wagon circle.

It was then that Mrs. Hennessey appeared, fully dressed and looking rather stubborn. If she felt any embarrassment she was hiding it under a firm stare of indignation. Barry was waiting for her, having seen to it that Conway and the others had drawn out of earshot.

"Make your choice, did you?" he asked with a casual smile.

She faltered for just a moment and then let a thin smile come to her lips. "Any reason why I shouldn't?"

"It's your affair. You generally seem to know what you're doing."

"I try. It seemed to me that I might do much worse than to take a chance on a man who seems to have so much under control."

"Then you think I'm licked?"

"Aren't you?"

He didn't like the way she put it so he changed the subject. "Now what about Rossiter? What do you think happened to him?"

This time she dropped the show of defiance. "I honestly don't know. I was asleep. Before I could get myself fully awake I was all tied up. I don't know how many men did it."

"And you didn't hear any sounds or talk?"

"Practically none. There was a movement of the wagon as though a struggle might be taking place. No more than that. I think Mr. Rossiter must have been caught by surprise as I was."

Barry wanted to ask whether she thought Rossiter had been equally naked but decided that it wasn't quite the question for this particular moment.

"Better get yourself some breakfast," he advised. "If you feel up to it. The men are out searching now."

"Your men?"

"No. They left for Fort Laramie a good hour before dawn."

There was clear suspicion in her eyes as she demanded, "Are you sure you don't know anything about this, Sergeant?"

"I'm sure."

She frowned a little. "I think I believe you. But I've got a feeling that you could be making some pretty close guesses."

"Save the guesses until we find Rossiter," he told her. "Maybe we won't need to guess."

"And you think he will be found? Alive?"

"I'm afraid so. Seems like there wasn't anybody around had any better reason to want him dead than I did, and I didn't have anything to do with what happened to him. Now what about your ideas on the subject? Was there anybody who might have been riled up a bit because you decided to play house with the fat slob?" He purposely framed his questions in terms that might irritate her.

She refused to be irritated. "No one," she said firmly.

He remembered that Ben Samuels had been paying quite a lot of attention to her but he didn't mention the fact. Somehow he felt pretty sure that Samuels had been just behind Corporal Wirtz when the squad left the camp. It didn't necessarily mean anything but he also recalled that he hadn't been able to locate either Ladou or Sawdust in the group.

"Get some breakfast," he repeated as he turned away. "Maybe we'll know something before long."

CHAPTER 17

He found Addison backing cautiously out of his wagon, Linda protesting and helping at the same time.

"You are thoroughly unsatisfactory invalids, both of you!" she told them. Then, almost without a pause, she asked, "What happened over there, Tom? What was Mrs. Hennessey doing in Rossiter's wagon?"

Barry shook his head, keeping his face straight partly because the unwary head movement brought pain. "She wasn't doing anything when we found her. She was all tied up. I didn't ask what she might have been doing earlier."

He let her show her impatience at his reply and then went on to tell what he knew about the affair. It was fun to watch Linda's face. The girl couldn't decide whether to be shocked at Mrs. Hennessey's behavior or annoyed that the enemy should have gained a recruit. The fact that Rossiter was missing didn't seem to interest her at all.

Addison took it more seriously. "Mighty strange that this happens just as your—our—men are leaving camp. Do you think there's a connection?"

Barry didn't intend to commit himself to anything just because the Lieutenant had seemed to accept some of the responsibility. "I don't see what connection there would be," he said shortly.

"I do. Your friend Sawdust may have felt that he would be doing you a good turn to punish Rossiter for that shooting attempt which I'm sure Rossiter ordered."

"Not likely, Lieutenant. This could be serious, kidnapping or maybe even murder. Sawdust wouldn't tangle me—or himself—in that kind of thing."

Linda asked quietly, "Has anyone searched the wagon?"

"No. Your father said that Rossiter's clothes were still there. That was about all he had time to see before Mrs. Hennessey chased everybody out."

"Too bad you had that hole in your neck!" she snapped. "I'm sure she would have let *you* stay and help her!"

"Now, Melinda Jessie! Don't talk like that."

"And don't call me . . . oh, forget it! What I'm trying to get you to see is that there might have been another reason back of this. The trouble is that you can't get your mind past Mrs. Hennessey and the way she was wrapped in that blanket."

"Unwrapped in the blanket," Barry corrected.

"Shut up! Last night I overheard something about your men needing extra revolvers. It happens that Abe Shingle had two brand new Navy Colts. I could easily guess that they planned to knock Rossiter on the head while they stole those guns. What they didn't expect was that they would find somebody else in the wagon. Maybe they were a little rattled at what they found. Anyway they tied up Mrs. Hennessey and took Rossiter away so he couldn't raise an alarm."

"They were rattled, all right," he agreed. "It would have been more fun to tie up Rossiter and take Katie."

"You have a low mind."

He grinned happily at her tone. This wasn't the way she had sounded when they had gotten into a real quarrel. "You could be right on both counts. But don't spread that theory.

Let's wait and see what happens."

They heard even wilder theories while they ate breakfast, Katie Hennessey offering a few. She didn't seem at all embarrassed at what had happened and she was offering no excuses to anyone. The meal was just about over when the militiamen came into camp with a battered edition of Herbert Rossiter. They had found him barefooted and in his nightshirt some little distance south of the wagon trace. He had a black eye, badly bruised feet, a few odd scratches and a couple of badly scraped knees. There was also a knob on the back of his head and he was shivering painfully in the forty degree chill even though one of the militiamen had thrown a blanket around him. He could still use his voice, however. He was accusing Barry of everything before he even hit the ground.

Then he successively named Conway, Ben Samuels, Addison, and the Cheyennes as the guilty parties. He didn't ask about Katie Hennessey even though the woman had slipped away at his approach. He simply ranted, leaving everyone well aware that he was too angry to make much sense.

Coffee well laced with brandy took some of the chill out of him but his story still didn't amount to much. All he could say for certain—between wild accusations—was that he must have been hit on the head while he slept. He knew nothing of what had happened in the wagon; the first thing he remembered was that he was tied across a saddle, hands and feet lashed together under the animal's belly. It was dark and he could see nothing but he believed that another horse was ahead of the one he was riding so unhappily. He tried to shout but nobody paid any attention to him.

Finally, when he thought that he would break in half, there was a halt. Two muffled figures appeared beside him. He thought that they had sacks or something over their heads because he could see no shapes or faces. And they had not uttered a word. One of them simply cut the ropes which held him. The other lifted his feet and let him fall on his head to the ground.

After that he was not too sure of events. One man had picked him up and the other had punched him in the eye. They picked him up again but this time they aimed him back down the ridge on which they had been riding, a hard boot starting him on his return journey. He could hear his captors riding away but he had not been able to see them. He had started running to keep warm but the rocky ground had cut his feet and twice he had fallen hard. He thought he must have struggled along for perhaps half a mile before daylight came to give him a proper direction. The scouts had found him exhausted.

"It was those savages of Barry's!" he almost shouted at the end of his tale. "No better than Cheyennes, any of them!"

"Wait a bit," Barry put in quietly. "You've got no reason to accuse anybody. You didn't see the men. You said so yourself."

The fat man stormed again, weakly but with plenty of rage to make up for weakness. Then Addison broke in. "According to your story, Mr. Rossiter, this attack must have taken place a little more than an hour before daybreak. You were a prisoner until perhaps a half hour before dawn."

"They had me longer than that!"

"All the better for the point I'm trying to make. Our men left this camp just about one hour before dawn. I looked at my watch when they reported out. By your own account you were riding with your captors at that moment. I'm afraid you'll have to find someone else to charge."

Barry let the Lieutenant handle it. He was pretty certain that Addison had actually seen no watch in the darkness when the squad left but the time was about what he said it was. Maybe the Lieutenant thought he was telling substantial truth. Maybe he didn't know that Ladou and Featherstone had not been with the other men. Barry certainly didn't propose to tell him.

They finally managed to get Rossiter to his wagon, Katie Hennessey moving in to take care of him. He didn't bother to ask what had happened to her but she didn't seem to mind the slight. Evidently she had thrown in her lot with him in spite of his disposition.

Addison managed to ride across to the telegraph station again before the train pulled out but he had nothing important to mention when he came back. Mostly the talk was about the Chivington raid. The claims of victory were getting bigger all the time and the settlers were celebrating as though they had taken some personal part in it.

It was only when Addison and Barry were back in the wagon once more, both quite willing to play invalids after their morning excitement, that the Lieutenant asked, "Do you think your pet bandits pulled that trick this morning, Barry? I understand how they would feel, and they asked about getting revolvers."

"I don't think I'll offer any guesses, sir. If they'd wanted me to know about it they'd have told me."

"Have it your own way. Personally, I think Miss Conway called it the way it happened. Officially, I'm completely mystified."

"That's fine sir."

They halted that night near another scrubby settlement where a bored private stood guard over a telegraph station. Addison reported once more and again came up with information that the Chivington affair was arousing considerable enthusiasm. Colorado authorities claimed that they had squelched the Indian uprising completely. There was even a rumor that Chivington's men had killed a Confederate agent in the Cheyenne village.

Rossiter and Katie ate their suppers in some seclusion. The man seemed to have recovered quite rapidly, his injuries no more than superficial. He even exerted himself to walk across toward Barry when the company was getting ready to turn in for the night. Glaring through his one good eye he snarled, "I'll make you sweat for this, damn you! I know you're responsible."

Barry aimed an easy grin at him. "Odd coincidence. I know that you sent Shingle to murder me. Neither of us can prove it. Funny, eh?"

"I'll prove it!" Rossiter snapped. "I'll find a way."

"Such as by bribing a witness? Like you bribed a clerk to put my name on a casualty list? Mister, you're in one hell of a bad way to go around making threats so get out of here before I black that other eye of yours!"

He let his tone change from wry humor to harsh anger so fast that Rossiter flinched. The fat man didn't even reply. He simply turned and lurched toward Mrs. Hennessey and the wagon.

Next morning there was another early alarm. This time it was one of the men reporting that three horses had disappeared. Barry listened for some minutes before risking the pains of movement, learning as he listened that the missing animals were not draft horses. There was a moment for him to guess at the meaning of it but then someone shouted the explanation. The Rossiter wagon was empty. Completely empty of passengers this time.

The camp went into another flurry of excitement, finally working out the details. Conway found a note inside the wagon which had originally been Shingle's. It instructed him to act for the partnership in Denver, holding himself accountable for all partnership funds to be realized from sales. Rossiter simply stated that he would go back east now that the Indian danger was ended. He did not mention Mrs. Hennessey or his reason for leaving.

"No question about what he's got in mind," Conway growled. "He knows we're on to him so he's headed back to hide his tracks as best he can. He'll get rid of any evidence that you could have used and maybe steal me blind at the same time."

"You've got this train load of goods," Barry pointed out.

"It's small stuff compared to what we left back along the Ohio. A man with Rossiter's nerve will probably try to make me share up with him on this deal while he robs me of everything he left behind. And maybe he can get away with it. He's had plenty of experience and he's got quite a hold on the various officials he has bribed in the past."

"What about mail? Or telegraph? Can't you forestall him? It's already well into December. He could be delayed a long while by winter weather."

"I'll try. Somehow I don't think it's going to do much good."

Addison used the telegraph once more before the train pulled out, passing a personal message to Captain Pritchard. There probably was nothing that the army could do but it didn't hurt to pass the word.

For Barry the whole thing seemed hopeless. Conway evidently didn't think that Rossiter could be stopped. Barry was in an even worse position. He had no chance of making a journey east and he had no way of exerting any influence on his own behalf. Apparently Katie Hennessey had put her money on the right horse!

The wagons reached Denver three days before Christmas, the weather remaining better than fair although there were several light snow storms along the trail. Barry couldn't work up much interest in the town. For the Conways it would be the beginning of a new life but he didn't propose to make any claims on them or to pursue his personal affairs with Linda. A man who had nothing might as well face the facts. He was still an enlisted man, almost a prisoner. His future was Fort Laramie, at least for the coming winter. It didn't help his spirits much to know that his wound had healed almost completely during that final week of travel.

New orders awaited Addison when they reached Denver. The promised reinforcement for Fort Laramie had finally started west from the Missouri, the lateness of the season making it necessary for them to travel without much of a baggage train. Consequently several loads of blankets and other gear were being sent north out of Santa Fe. Addison was ordered to meet the wagons in Denver and to bring them on to Fort Laramie, using Barry as his guide. The assumption seemed to be that both men would be physically capable of handling the job.

"Where are the wagons now?" Conway asked when he was told about it.

Addison shook his head. "Nobody seems to know. That's the way the army seems to do things."

"I'll make you a deal. I need Barry to help me set up our new trading post. Leave him free for that chore and I'll provide both of you with quarters until your wagons show up."

"Fine with me. How about you, Sergeant?"

"It's got to be all right with him. He's a partner in this deal."

"I'm making no claims," Barry said briefly. "You know how . . ."

"All I know is that we had a deal. Things happened but I still need you. You're the one who knows the country. You're the one will have to tell me where we move and how." He grinned as he added, "And I've got two women who'll be in my hair if I don't handle it like that."

Christmas came on in a flurry of activity, with Barry putting in long hours at his new job. He could still feel an inner resentment at being so helpless to establish his own legitimate claims but it was good to know that the Conways wanted him and needed him. At his suggestion only two loads of flour were turned over to dealers at first, bringing good prices in spite of the fact that some of the edge had been taken off the market by an earlier supply that had come up from New Mexico. With the proceeds they paid off the teamsters who were not going to stay with the company and made down payments on a warehouse

and corral that would become headquarters for the operation. From that point they could sell the balance of the shipment at retail and take a larger profit at the same time that
they were letting the public know that the new company
was doing business.

Conway also used private funds to buy a small house for
his family, Addison and Barry setting up their quarters in
one of the empty wagons. For Barry the arrangement was
quite convenient. He was handy to his base of operations
as well as to the office in the warehouse. It was in that
office that Linda had taken over the keeping of company
books.

In a matter of three days a routine was getting pretty well
set up, even to Addison's frequent calls at the new office.
Mostly the Lieutenant was having plenty of difficulty in
getting around, particularly with the telegraph office some
distance from his living quarters, but he still managed to
see Linda several times a day. Barry couldn't be sure what
it meant and he didn't propose to ask questions.

Then the Fort Laramie wire reported that Rossiter had
lodged two charges against army personnel. He had
reached Fort Sedgwick and was making his presence
known. He claimed that one Sergeant Barry had been
involved in a shooting incident in which a man named
Shingle had been killed. According to him the affair had
been virtually a murder. He further stated that two Navy
Colts belonging to Shingle had been stolen by Privates
Featherstone and Samuels. Fort Laramie was asking Lieutenant Addison for his version and for any possible investigation.

"Smart bastard," Barry said in a low voice when Addison

told him of the wire. "He's figuring to keep us on the defensive as long as he can."

Addison nodded. Of late he had seemed to speak as one of the group, his understanding of both the Barry and the Conway affairs making it easy for him to think as one of them. "I'd say he still was making guesses about that little party the boys threw for him. You notice he names Featherstone and Samuels. I think he just hated them the most. My guess is that Featherstone and Ladou did the job."

Barry knew better than to commit himself on that point. Officers were officers, no matter what else might be said about them. A man who had served in the ranks for three years couldn't forget the point.

CHAPTER 18

Conway, Addison, and Barry worked out the draft of the wire that went back in reply. It read:

JESSE CONWAY, PARTNER OF ROSSITER, STATES ROSSITER IS THIEF AND LIAR. SHINGLE KILLED IN SELF DEFENSE. MURDER CHARGE SHOULD BE ATTEMPTED MURDER BY SHINGLE. NO KNOWL-EDGE OF MISSING GUNS. DEATHS OF PRIVATES PEACE, BRADY AND O'CONNELL LARGELY DUE TO ROSSITER TREACHERY. PROPOSE TO MAKE OFFICIAL CHARGES TO THAT EFFECT.
signed
ADDISON.

"Maybe we're a little late in trying to spike his guns," the

Lieutenant growled, "but we'll sure as hell give it a try."

That same day the tone of gossip in town seemed to change. The continuing celebration over Chivington's victory began to turn sour. Fresh reports had come in which stated bluntly that the affair had been no more than a massacre of women, children and old men. There were rumors that the Cheyennes were gathering neighboring tribes for a winter campaign in retaliation.

Barry paid it little heed. Part of the time he was busy with his work at the new trading post where the balance of the shipment was now being sold directly by the new company. With Linda helping out in the office work it gave him a chance to be with her much of the time, their relationship still a little strained but on reasonably friendly terms.

In late afternoon there was a reply from Laramie. Captain Pritchard made it a personal message to Lieutenant Addison. Privates Featherstone and Samuels did not have Navy Colts in their possession. The whole affair was being held up because the wire had gone out again. Nothing had been heard from Fort Sedgwick or Julesburg since early morning. The last message through had carried the story of Rossiter's complaint along with the account of how Congress was bucking President Lincoln's plan to give Tennessee, Arkansas and Louisiana their statehood once more. The first move had been to refuse recognition of the electors those states had picked in the recent presidential election. Evidently it was not going to be easy for Confederates to regain Federal citizenship or even state citizenship.

Barry shrugged when he heard about it. "What difference does it make to me. I can't go east where I might want to establish myself so as to be heard in court. Another obstacle won't make any difference."

"Maybe I could make the try," Conway told him. "I had a letter waiting for me when I arrived. I didn't tell you about it because I wasn't sure but what it would raise false hopes. The fact is that Rossiter's under investigation at the Cairo base. Our agent there got wind of what was happening and changed as much company property as possible to my name alone. So far the dodge has worked. We don't know what it will mean but there's a chance that any property Rossiter has owned or partly owned may be tied up."

"You mean you'd beat your way east with winter coming on?"

Conway grinned. "You'd go if you could."

"Who takes care of this place? I'll be moving north to join my fellow outcasts before long."

"Let it go," Conway told him with a wry smile. "We'll see what I can learn by mail or wire."

They went back to work while Addison used the small carriage Conway had bought for general use and went back to the telegraph office. It was well that he did. Within the next three hours the wire was hot. So was local gossip.

The first report was that the supply wagons from Santa Fe were one day south of Denver. Then came a wire from Fort Laramie to the effect that further search had disclosed two Navy revolvers in the possession of Corporal Wirtz and Trooper Welland. Addison was asked to verify the statements the men had made that they had purchased the weapons personally. The gossip was due to the change of feeling about the Chivington raid. No longer were people boasting that their militia had settled the Indian threat for a long time to come. Now they were passing the report that

Chivington had attacked a village of friendly Indians when no warriors were at home. The affair had been nothing but a massacre of women, children and old men.

"I'll say one thing for Chivington," Barry commented dryly. "If he hit a village that didn't have any warriors in it he didn't hit friendlies. We know where the warriors were and what they were doing. Give the devil his due."

"It doesn't alter the situation," Addison told him soberly. "Word is out that the Sioux and Cheyenne are definitely joined up for war. Private Featherstone called the turn, all right."

"What about Featherstone and his little playmates?" Barry asked. "How are you going to answer that wire about the guns?"

Addison laughed. "I've already answered it. In a sneaky kind of way, perhaps. I wired Captain Pritchard that I was positive that the weapons now in the possession of the men named had not been the property of Abe Shingle. Somehow I feel pretty certain that Rossiter owned the man, body, soul, and guns."

Barry's chuckle became a full laugh. "Lieutenant, you have definitely been contaminated. You're getting to be as shifty as the rest of us."

Addison beamed as though he had just been awarded a medal. "I owe Rossiter nothing except a couple of wounds and three dead men on my conscience. And I'm going back to Fort Laramie where I may have to depend on that gang of yours for a lot of things. I guess I can use my head once in a while!"

"What about the wagons? Are you figuring to keep them rolling?"

"Why not? We've been lucky about winter weather so far. No point in wasting time with the snow season already overdue. We'll move on toward Laramie as soon as we can make it."

Barry nodded. "I'd better find Jess Conway and tell him. He'll want to look over some of the things I've been handling."

Addison's smile had turned a little out of balance as he suggested, "You'd better tell Linda while you're at it. I judge that you have a bit of unfinished business there also."

When it was clear that he didn't intend to say more Barry went on across to the warehouse-office. Linda was alone at her desk. She gave him a smile as he entered but then turned to her work again.

He stood silent for a moment or two but then broke in to tell her about his imminent departure. "So it's back to the wilds," he concluded. "Sorry things didn't work out better."

"What do you mean? Things are working out perfectly."

"Not for me. I don't intend to take any kind of partnership on a charity basis. I've been mighty happy to help you folks get started but I don't figure that any part of this is mine."

"Couldn't you call it ours?" she asked quietly.

He looked up quickly, liking what he saw in the dark eyes. "Once I hoped it would be that way. But that was a long time ago—before you decided that you wouldn't marry a rebel."

She was still meeting his glance when she asked, "Did I ever say that I wouldn't marry you?"

"Maybe not, exactly. It seems to me that you called me a

traitor, an ingrate, a tool of slave interests, an idiot, a pig-headed secessionist, a miserable rebel, a . . ."

"But I didn't say I wouldn't marry you."

He was trying hard to keep the grin from breaking loose. "Sorry," he told her in his most abject tones. "I must have misunderstood. Probably a bit thin-skinned because of those little pet names. I jumped at conclusions."

"Are you still too angry to jump back?"

"You know the answer to that, I think."

"Well, tell me! I've practically proposed to you. I think the least you can do in return is to ease my pride a little and tell me that you want it that way."

He was gathering her into his arms before she even finished the little speech. Somehow it didn't seem possible that more than three years had passed since they had last embraced. In one way it had been like a lifetime but still it seemed like no time at all.

He said as much, adding, "There's still a problem of time. I'll be moving north to be gone all winter. No telling how much longer."

"I'll wait. This time I'll know why I'm waiting."

There was another interval of silence when neither of them thought it necessary to speak but then Linda asked, "Will there be danger on this trip?"

"No more than anywhere else in this country. There shouldn't be any Indian problem even with the new uprisings east of here. Snow will cause us some trouble, I suppose, but we'll be following the telegraph line most of the way. The trail will be kept pretty well broken. It won't be too bad."

He took her in his arms again. "Forget the details. We've

got a lot of catching up to do."

Neither of them heard the door open. Finally it was Addison's voice that broke in on their concentration. "That ought to keep you warm all the way to Laramie, Sergeant. Can you break it up long enough to hear what the latest wire told me?"

The pair separated in some embarrassment but then Linda came back quickly to put an arm about Barry's waist. He knew that it was a sort of gesture of defiance but he liked it. Trying to keep his own voice casual, he asked, "Are you going to tell me that we don't go to Fort Laramie after all?"

"No. On that score you're not so lucky. Our message reports that a Cheyenne chief named Spotted Tail led a surprise raid on Julesburg some days ago, apparently in retaliation for the Chivington raid. Part of the town was burned. Many of the inhabitants fled to the protection of Fort Sedgwick where they were in a state of siege for some time. That was when the telegraph went dead, apparently.

"The chief casualties were a group of miners preparing to move east from Julesburg. They had assembled a train and were about to risk the bad weather when the Cheyennes struck. The report is that the entire train was wiped out. It included two people who had just joined it. The man was Herbert Rossiter. Nobody seems to know the woman's name."

The elder Conways came hurrying into the office then, both looking a little disappointed when they realized that Addison had preceded them with the word about Rossiter.

"I guess we won't need to worry about what will happen back east," Jesse said after a bit of hesitation. "Seems like a man oughtn't to be glad over what a bunch of savages did but this time I ain't going to pretend that I'm not kinda glad."

Mrs. Conway had recovered a little more rapidly. While her husband stumbled through his remarks she stared hard at the way her daughter was holding fast to Barry. There was a trace of smile at the corners of her mouth as she asked, "Are you two celebrating the occasion or has there been something a little more personal happening?"

"You could call it personal," Barry told her, keeping his own expression casually genial. "I decided that I wanted a fine lady like you for a mother-in-law. The only way I could manage it was by marrying your only daughter. So I guess I'll have to. . . ."

He never did get around to saying the rest of it. Linda kicked him on the shin.

Center Point Publishing
600 Brooks Road ● PO Box 1
Thorndike ME 04986-0001 USA

(207) 568-3717

US & Canada:
1 800 929-9108